Midnight Destiny

By

Ellen Dugan

Other titles by Ellen Dugan

THE LEGACY OF MAGICK SERIES

Legacy Of Magick, Book 1

Secret Of The Rose, Book 2

Message Of The Crow, Book 3

Beneath An Ivy Moon, Book 4

Under The Holly Moon, Book 5

The Hidden Legacy, Book 6

Spells Of The Heart, Book 7

Sugarplums, Spells & Silver Bells, Book 8

Magick & Magnolias, Book 9

Mistletoe & Ivy, Book 10

Cake Pops, Charms & Do No Harm, Book 11

Wish Upon The Moon, Book 12 (Coming 2022)

THE GYPSY CHRONICLES

Gypsy At Heart, Book 1

Gypsy Spirit, Book 2

DAUGHTERS OF MIDNIGHT SERIES

Midnight Gardens, Book 1

Midnight Masquerade, Book 2

Midnight Prophecy, Book 3

Midnight Star, Book 4

Midnight Secrets, Book 5

Midnight Destiny, Book 6

HEMLOCK HOLLOW TRILOGY

Hemlock Lane, Book 1

Wolfsbane Ridge, Book 2

Nightshade Court, Book 3

HEMLOCK HOLLOW ANTHOLOGY

Bewitched in Hemlock Hollow, Book 1

Beguiled in Hemlock Hollow, Book 2 (Coming 2022)

ACKNOWLEDGMENTS

As always, thanks to my family, friends, beta readers, and editors. A special thanks to my two-year-old granddaughter, Kenzie. I babysat her full time for four and a half months this year as the pandemic shook the world, while her parents waited for an opening at a good daycare. She reminded me what it's like to care for a strong-willed toddler full time. I spent a good amount of time laughing at toddler shenanigans and the rest of the time trying to keep up with her.

The scene where Danielle eats dirt and rocks and then chomps down on Estella when she tries to get the rocks out of her mouth was inspired by real events. I had a bruise that lasted for two days from my darling girl's teeth. I guess she showed me.

You don't find love, it finds you,

It's got a little bit to do with destiny, fate and what's written in the stars.

-Anaïs Nin

CHAPTER ONE

The kicky breeze that whipped through the cottage gardens of the Marquette mansion was a sure sign of change. There was the slightest chill in the September air, a welcome signal that the summer had at last caved in to fall. I lifted my face to the fresh air and breathed it in.

I walked along with my eighteen-month-old niece, Danielle, and considered all of the changes in my life. It had been a year since I had tossed my belongings in a duffle bag, hopped on a plane, and flown clear across the country to meet the family I'd never known I had. The culture shock from coming from California and moving to a historic—and haunted—small town had been huge.

Twelve months later I felt right at home, more than I ever had bopping around the world as an Air Force brat. Who would've thought that I, Estella Flores Midnight, would end up in Illinois living in a spooky little village? However, I wasn't on my own. It still surprised me to wake up and realize I had a grandmother, three sisters, three brothers-in-law, a nephew, and nieces. Oh, and a cousin. The wish I'd made on my birthday the year before had come true.

I had a family, a big one, and I wasn't alone. Not anymore.

While the baby toddled, I followed her around making sure she didn't get into too much trouble. The kid was a pistol. She darted here and there, exclaiming over every flower and every leaf she saw. I didn't dare take my eyes off her, because the kid was strong-willed and she'd already thrown a fit when I'd stopped her from finding out what the gravel on the path tasted like.

"Lala *look*!" Danielle held up a fallen oak leaf like a prize.

Lala was Danielle's version of saying Estella. I thought it was hilarious. "That's pretty," I said as she toddled over to me. I knew the drill by now. Crouching down to her level, I inspected the treasure with all the respect an eighteen-month-old would expect.

"Dat's pe-tty," Danielle agreed.

I took a moment and straightened up her tiny brown pigtails. Danielle allowed it, but I knew better than to fuss over her hair too long.

"Floweys!" she exclaimed, taking off to go pat the chrysanthemums blooming at the edge of the path.

"Yup," I agreed. "There are lots of flowers." I tried not to wince when she grabbed handfuls of blooms and yanked them free. There was a wedding scheduled to be held in the gardens this weekend, and I'd promised Gabriella I'd keep her daughter out of the perennial beds.

While Danielle bust a gut laughing over her 'floweys,' I sat on the edge of the grass. Worst case scenario, I decided, I'd pop over to Max's nursery and buy a few more mum plants to replace the ones Danielle was scalping. She was having way too much fun grabbing flower heads and bringing them over to me. In a few minutes I had quite the collection decorating the legs of my jeans.

Honestly, I doubted Gabriella would even notice. My sister had a lot more on her mind than worrying over a few scalped chrysanthemums. I heard footsteps on the gravel path and turned my head. When I saw who it was, my heart gave one hard thud in reaction.

Danielle looked up as well, and when she spotted her uncle, she grinned. "Cee-cee!" was toddler-speak for *Chauncey,* and Danielle promptly abandoned me to race toward him.

Chauncey stood waiting on the path, and as soon as she reached him, he grabbed her and tossed her high in the air. Danielle's delighted screams filled the garden, and as I watched them both grin at each other, I was hit all over again with how damn hot he was.

He was tall with a lean build and a head full of dark tousled hair. His sexy man-scruff and the light of humor in his dark eyes...it was a hell of a package.

I ought to be used to it by now. But the truth was, for

the past year I'd been fighting my attraction to him. *We aren't well suited for each other,* I reminded myself for the thousandth time. We had nothing in common—not our backgrounds or our lifestyles. Yet I still wanted him.

To make matters worse, he'd clearly put me in the buddy category. Which made my secret physical reaction to him extremely embarrassing. The man didn't have a clue as to how I felt...and I intended to keep it that way.

I was determined to get over my desire for him. Somehow. I dug down deep and went for a casual tone of voice. "Hey," I said, while he walked over carrying Danielle.

"Hi, Aunt Lala." He glanced down at the chrysanthemums. "Weren't you supposed to keep Danielle out of the flowers while you babysat?"

"We were pruning a bit," I said nonchalantly. "Tidying up the place."

Chauncey grinned at the lie. "I can always run up to the garden center and buy a couple new plants before the wedding ceremony."

I nodded. "That's exactly what I was thinking."

Danielle squirmed to be put down and Chauncey set her on her feet. The toddler immediately went right back to picking more flowers and bringing them to me.

"Have you heard anything yet?" Chauncey asked.

"Nope." I slid my phone from my pocket. "They've only been gone a couple of hours. The doctor's appointment was at two o'clock."

Chauncey sat beside me on the grass and Danielle started bringing him flowers as well. "I guess we'll find out soon enough."

"I bet Gabriella's pregnant," I said. "She was green around the gills when they left for their appointment."

Chauncey grinned. "I think so too. Philippe told me Gabriella was really sick for the first few months she carried that little monster over there."

"Who's a monster, *mija*?" I asked with a playful growl in my voice.

"Lala!" Danielle whipped her head around and ran straight at me, with a growl of her own.

I absorbed the toddler tackle and let her think she'd knocked me over. "Oh no!" My voice was breathy and high as I rolled over with her on the grass. "Somebody save me from the monster!"

"I'll save you!" Chauncey's voice had me jolting and Danielle laughing.

Now, I not only had an armful of toddler, but Chauncey Marquette had grabbed me off the ground and picked us both up. Danielle thought it was great and her laughter rolled out across the gardens. As for me, finding myself suddenly in his arms had the laughter dying in my throat.

The last thing I'd ever expected was for Chauncey to join in on the play. Now I was held close to his chest, like some heroine from a sappy romance novel. When he grinned down at me, my heart almost stopped all together.

He wiggled his eyebrows. "You're supposed to say: 'My hero.'"

It took me a moment, but I managed to roll my eyes at him. "I don't think Danielle knows those words, yet."

"My Cee-Cee!" Danielle shouted.

"That's close enough," he decided and put us both down.

I let Danielle slide out of my arms, and my eyes were helplessly locked on his. Fortunately for me, as soon as her feet hit the ground, she was off and racing across the grass.

"I...I guess..." I winced over hearing myself stammer. *Get ahold of yourself!* I thought. "I'd better go and make sure she doesn't get into any trouble." I took a step back.

Chauncey stood absolutely still. "You probably should."

Something had changed. The vibes in the garden had shifted from playful to something else. Whatever it was had heat rising to my face, and my heart slamming against my ribs. My mouth went bone dry, and nervously, I licked my lips.

His eyes narrowed at the movement, and suddenly there was a look on his face. One I'd not seen before…

"I should go," I said again, inwardly cursing over sounding like a moron. "I'll, uh...see you around, Chauncey."

"See you," he said.

My face flushed, I took off after Danielle who'd shot across the lawn in search of new adventures. I absolutely refused to look over my shoulder to see if he was watching me. I had more pride than that.

I caught up to the toddler who was now pointing at a bird on a tree branch, and pride be damned, I glanced back anyway. The man was strolling down the garden path, his hands tucked in the pockets of his slacks, seemingly without a care in the world...while I stood there with my palms sweating and my heart racing.

"Damn it," I muttered. "I can put a man twice my size in a controlled hold. I can handle mean drunks in a bar. But every time Chauncey Marquette gets too close, I make a fool out of myself."

I'd known him for a year; my sister was married to his half-brother. I'd laughed with him and helped take care of him when he'd been hurt. We'd attended weddings and family functions together, and I even danced with him. Twice.

We'd kissed once, too. *But did that even count?* I wondered. Probably not, since we'd both been possessed by a couple of horny ghosts at the time... Now we were friends, I supposed, and godparents to the adorable monster currently trying to climb up my leg.

I swung the baby up in my arms and dropped a kiss on her cheek. "What is it, Danielle," I said, "that makes me think that Chauncey Marquette might be my destiny?"

"Cookie?" Danielle asked hopefully.

I pressed a kiss to her hair. "Sure, *mija,* let's go get you a cookie."

I carried her back to the family wing of the house and wished that all desires could be so easily satisfied.

***

I was sitting with Danielle in the kitchen when I heard that Gabriella and Philippe had finally come home. Danielle was plowing through her supper in her high chair, and I was supervising, since she was determined to feed herself.

My sister and her husband were speaking quietly as they came up the steps to the second floor of the family's wing. Hearing their hushed voices, my stomach dropped.

Something was wrong.

They'd been gone for almost four hours, and I was more than a little concerned. I hadn't texted them because I knew if there'd been a true emergency, they would have contacted me right away. However, I could feel the stressed-out vibes before they even started down the hall. Bracing myself for bad news, I turned to them as they walked into the room.

They were arm in arm and Gabriella was leaning heavily against Philippe. "We're back," Gabriella said. She was the palest I'd ever seen her.

"Hey, guys," I said.

"Mama, Dada!" Danielle shouted in joy and waved

her hands.

Philippe smiled at his daughter but assisted Gabriella into a kitchen chair. He pressed a kiss to the top of her head, went straight to the fridge, and pulled out a can of ginger ale. Silently, he popped the top and handed it to his wife.

Gabriella let her purse drop beside her chair. She took the soft drink and chugged it. I sat silently and waited while she gulped down most of the can. Eventually she came up for air.

My sister let loose a loud burp and grimaced. "Better," she said.

"Gabriella, are you okay?" I asked.

With a sigh Gabriella leaned back in her chair and shut her eyes. "Do you want the good news, the bad news, or the *holy crap* news?"

"Tell me," I said, getting more worried by the minute.

Philippe rested his hand on Gabriella's shoulder. "The good news is that we are pregnant."

I smiled. "That's great!"

"The bad news is that her doctor says Gabriella was dehydrated from her morning sickness, so we had to go to the emergency department for an IV. Which is why we were gone for so long."

"Is it that super bad morning sickness?" I asked. "Hyper-something?"

"Hyperemesis gravidarum," Philippe answered. "The doctor is concerned that it might be. Gabriella has been told to rest and push the fluids as much as possible for the time being."

"Oh," I said.

"Rest." Gabriella grimaced. "How am I supposed to stay in bed when I have a toddler running amuck all over the mansion and we're finishing up the renovation of the attic?"

"*Ma belle*," Philippe said. "We will find a way."

"It's next to impossible," Gabriella said, as tears rolled down her face.

"We will do whatever is necessary for your health and the safety of the babies," Philippe said to her.

"*Babies*?" I did a double take. "Did you say babies —as in more than one?"

"And the holy crap news is," Gabriella said, "that we're having twins."

I jumped out of my chair and ran to her. "Oh my god, that's wonderful!" I threw my arms around her shoulders and gave her a squeeze.

But instead of laughing with joy or smiling, my sister broke down. "I'm so scared," she said, sobbing on my shoulder.

As if in sympathy, Danielle began to cry in her highchair. Philippe picked up the baby, while I held onto my sister and rubbed her back. "You know the family will be happy to help you, Gabriella."

Gabriella sniffled. "I can't impose on them. Camilla has her shop and her new family; Drusilla and Garrett are still settling in with the children. Dru went through so much on the road to adoption, I can't intrude on what should be a happy time for them."

"I'll hire a nanny, and a live-in nurse for you, if necessary, until the morning sickness passes," Philippe added.

Gabriella sat back and wiped at her face. "As much as I don't like the thought of a nanny, or a nurse, lying in the emergency room and getting an IV has made me realize that I don't have much say in this matter anymore."

"We will do whatever we need to do to increase our chances of a successful outcome to this pregnancy," Philippe said firmly.

"That's exactly right." I nodded. "Philippe's right."

He grinned. "That's what I'm always telling her."

"I don't like the thought of strangers living with us," Gabriella said as more tears began to fall.

"You don't need to hire a nanny," I said, patting her back. "Not when you've got me and Gran. We can tag-team, or I can move in here for a few months and help with Danielle."

"But Estella." Gabriella shook her head. "I can't ask you to give up your life for the next few months. Your jobs—"

"Shut up, Gabriella," I said firmly. "I work part time with Cammy at her shop, and part time for Garrett at the winery show room. As both of my bosses are *family*, I'm sure they'll be flexible and give me some time off for a while."

Gabriella blew out a shaky breath. "It's just that I—"

"I'm not giving up anything." I grabbed a paper towel from the roll on the counter and handed it to her. "Here, mop up your face with this."

"Thanks." She accepted it.

"Suck it up buttercup," I said. "You'll simply have to get used to me being underfoot until you feel better."

She wiped her eyes. "But with all the renovations, we're currently in the guest room, and our old room is still a construction zone. Where would you even sleep?"

I shrugged. "Toss a sleeping bag on the floor for me in Danielle's room. I'll be fine."

Philippe gave my ponytail a tug. "I believe we can do better than that. There's plenty of room in the nursery. I'll have the guest bed taken out of storage and brought in for you."

"Whatever is easiest, Philippe," I said. "You don't have to fuss."

"I'll damn well make sure that you are comfortable if you stay with us for an extended period of time!" Gabriella's voice rose.

"Okay, okay," I said soothingly. "When was the last time you ate? You're awfully grouchy."

Gabriella rubbed a hand over her forehead. "I don't remember. I had a piece of toast this morning before the dry heaves hit."

I went to their fridge, pulled out slices of Colby-jack cheese, and grabbed a sleeve of crackers from the cabinet. "Can you handle a snack?" I asked.

"I don't know," Gabriella grumped.

I handed her a cracker. "Take a nibble. See how it sits."

While Gabriella tried a cracker, Philippe went off to change Danielle. He sent me a worried look over his wife's head, and I gave him a nod, letting him know that I'd keep an eye on her. Straightening my shoulders, I pulled out the chair and sat down next to my sister at the kitchen table.

"So..." I began in an effort to make my sister smile. "They decided since you were so pale and twice as cranky as usual, that it had to be twins?"

Gabriella gave me a look. "No, I was bigger than expected, so they did an ultrasound, and there they were."

"Do you have pictures?" I asked.

"In my purse." Gabriella pointed to her bag that she'd dropped on the floor.

"Can I look?"

"Sure." She reached for a square of cheese, sniffed it, and then tasted it.

I fished the roll of photos out and Gabriella pointed out each of the fetuses in the ultrasound images. I had to grin over the *Baby A* and *Baby B* markings on the pictures.

"This is so cool," I said. "I mean...just *look* at them."

"It still hasn't quite hit home," Gabriella admitted in a shaking voice.

"Gran's going to flip," I said, unable to wipe the

smile off my face.

"The cheese tastes good," Gabriella said, taking another cautious bite. "With Danielle all I could manage was fudgesicles and apples for a while."

I laughed. "That's the craziest combination I ever heard."

Gabriella wiped away fresh tears. "I'm so glad you're here. Philippe is scared, but he won't admit it, and I'm...well I'm completely overwhelmed and *terrified*. What if I miscarry? What if something is wrong with the babies? Do you know all the complications that go along with multiples? The things the doctor told us scared me to death. What if I—"

"What if purple elephants fall from the sky?" I cut her off and took her hand. "I'd take this one day and one week at a time, Gabriella. Otherwise, you'll make yourself a basket case."

Gabriella sighed. "You're right. Are you sure you want to do this? I mean you'll be giving up your personal life..."

I gave her an arch look. "You may not have noticed, as you were busy getting knocked up with twins, but I don't have much of a personal life."

Gabriella's lips twitched. "Okay if you're serious about this—the staying with us and helping with Danielle for a while—"

"I am," I assured her, giving her fingers a bolstering squeeze.

"All I ask is that you don't hover or treat me like I'm

an invalid." She nibbled on a square of cheese. "I suppose I'll have to slow down and try to relax. My blood pressure was elevated at the hospital."

I let go of her hand to help myself to a cracker. "Oh, yeah?"

She rolled her eyes. "I got a lecture about that too."

"*Mija*, I imagine any woman who is sick as a dog and told she's having twins has elevated blood pressure."

The barest glimmer of a smile hovered on her lips. "Thank you," she said. "I'm going to need that no nonsense honesty to counteract Philippe's hovering."

I patted her hand. "I've got you."

Gabriella took another bite of cheese. "I'm surprised the cheese is sitting okay on my stomach. Maybe because it's mild." She swallowed and burped.

"I'm going to get you some water," I said, rising and going to the cabinets. "I'm thinking that maybe you should limit the ginger ale. Cuz you belch like a frat boy, *Hermana.*"

"Yeah, I did that when I was pregnant with Danielle," she said. "I was a moody and mean bitch too."

"*What? You?*" Raising my eyebrows, I filled a glass with water and handed it to her. "I'm shocked to hear it. Normally you're all sweetness and light, like Dru."

Gabriella shot me a look over the rim of the glass.

"Trust me, Gabriella," I said, sitting again. "If you get too nasty with me, I'll put you in a controlled hold until you stop struggling, or until you pass out."

Gabriella began to laugh.

"Once your eyes roll up into your head and you're unconscious, I'll tuck you in bed and tell your husband that you are napping."

"Now you're making me nervous," she said.

"Look, I'm not much for sappy stuff, but I love you." I gave her a quick one-armed hug. "You need my help and I'm happy to lend a hand. It's as simple as that."

A few fresh tears rolled down her face. "I love you too, Estella. I'll never be able to repay you for helping us like this."

"Oh, well, I figure you can name one or *both* of the babies after me. That's a fair trade."

"If they're boys, that might be problematic," Gabriella pointed out.

"Nah," I said. "Go for some sort of celestial names. Besides, it'll make them tough. And don't worry, I'll teach *all* of your kids how to defend themselves. No punk from preschool will ever harass them."

At that moment, Chauncey popped his head in the kitchen. "Hi," he said carefully, noting the tears drying on Gabriella's too pale face.

Philippe was a few steps behind his brother, and Danielle took one look at her uncle and promptly threw herself at him. Chauncey automatically took the toddler, and she laid her head on his shoulder.

"What's going on?" Chauncey asked.

"There's some news," I said, keeping my arm around Gabriella's shoulder.

Gabriella sighed. "Tell him, Philippe."

"We're having twins," Philippe said.

"Holy shit!" Chauncey burst out.

"I couldn't have put it better myself," Gabriella said and then burped again.

CHAPTER TWO

The next afternoon I was packing my duffle bag and one of Dru's old suitcases for the big move up to the mansion. The family's calico, Mama Cat, sat on the chenille bedspread in my room and supervised.

"What do you think, kitty?" I asked the feline as she sniffed at the suitcase. "How crazy is it that I'll be living up in the old, haunted mansion?"

The cat yawned.

"Well, maybe you're used to the high life, having the run of this big old farmhouse, but I was only starting to get used to it, and now I'll be hanging out full time at the mansion for the foreseeable future." I folded a pumpkin-colored sweater into my duffle. "Promise me you'll keep an eye on Gran."

"It may shock you to know..." My grandmother's voice came from the hallway. "That I am more than capable of living on my own."

I lifted my head and smiled at my grandmother. She was still beautiful. Her ash-blonde hair swung to her chin and accented her blue eyes. Today she wore blue cotton cropped pants and a bright yellow top.

"Yeah, yeah." I pointed my finger at her. "Promise me, no wild parties while I'm gone, and no boys staying the night."

Gran sat on the bed. "Well, damn it," she said mildly. "I suppose I'll have to cancel the stripper pole I had ordered for the living room."

I burst out laughing. "Good one."

"This is a wonderful thing you're doing for your sister, Estella."

I shrugged. "Figured it's the least I could do," I said. "You all took me in last year and gave me a home. She needs help with Danielle until her morning sickness passes. I can do that."

"You know how stubborn Gabriella can be," my grandmother warned me. "You're going to have to watch her and make sure she rests. Knowing her, she'll find a way to have her computer in bed with her so she can work on her graphic design business."

"I can handle Gabriella," I said, closing the lid on the suitcase.

"It will be quiet with you gone," Gran said.

"You landed a bunch of new great-grandchildren in the past year," I said. "I'm sure between Brooke, Jaime, and Dru's little ones, they'll all keep you busy."

"I was going over to visit Drusilla and the children today and to stay for supper," Gran said, her face lighting up. "I'm so happy their adoption is final."

"They are great kids," I said, zipping up my duffle bag.

"Abby and Alex are still shy, but they seem to be growing more confident every day now," Gran agreed.

I took one last glance around my bedroom. It was spotless and looked like it did the first day I moved in. With a satisfied nod, I zipped up the second suitcase. "I can drop you off on my way to Gabriella's if you like," I said.

She smiled. "I'll take you up on that."

The family had given me the keys to the old pickup several months ago. It still ran like a top, even though it had more than a few rust spots. I dropped off Gran and ended up spending a few minutes with Dru and the kids.

Dru was in her element as a mother of three. First, she and Garrett had officially adopted Brooke right after their wedding, and then they had learned of a pair of young siblings who needed a permanent home. Drusilla and Garrett had worked their tails off to make it happen, and now the reward was a house full of family.

Alex was just shy of two and currently clung to Drusilla like a lifeline. She walked around the kitchen easily enough with the copper-haired toddler on her hip, while Brooke sat at their big sturdy farmhouse table with a pigtailed Abby, several pads of art paper, and big fat markers.

I pulled up a chair to see what they were working on.

"Hey, big sis," I said to thirteen-year-old Brooke.

The red-haired teen gave me a huge smile. "Abby and I are drawing pictures."

Abby was four with sandy blonde hair and very quiet. She gave me a timid smile and selected a marker with great care.

"Whatcha drawing, Abby?" I asked.

"My new house," she said.

I leaned closer to look. "Hey, that's pretty good! There's the widow's walk, and you drew in the flowers out front too."

Abby poked her tongue between her teeth in concentration and bent her head to her drawing.

"Are you moving up to the mansion today?" Brooke asked me.

"Yup," I said. "I'll need to get going here in a second."

Dru hitched the toddler up higher on her hip. "Please give Gabriella my best. Tell Philippe I'll put together a casserole or two and bring it over tomorrow. They can heat them up for supper whenever they like."

"Sure thing," I said to my sister. I stood, moved between the girls' chairs, and dropped a kiss on Brooke's head. "See ya around, *mi rosita*."

I saw Abby slant her eyes over toward me. My instinct had me giving her the same goodbye as Brooke. "See you later, *mija*."

Abby smiled. "Bye, Aunt Estella."

Her calling me "aunt" hit me right in the feels. She

and her brother had been living with Dru and Garrett for months now, while they went through the foster-to-adopt program, but she'd never called me *aunt* before.

Doing my best not to cry, I ran my hand over Alex's hair, patted Dru's shoulder, blew a kiss to Gran and let myself out. But then, making sure no one saw me, I wiped at my eyes.

That sweet little girl had broken my heart when I'd first met her. Her brown eyes were far too solemn for a child, and she'd had the hardest time adjusting to everything. I knew what it was like to be on your own with no family, and then suddenly in the middle of a loving and loud one. It was overwhelming, but it made me so damn happy to see that Abby was settling in.

Backing out of the driveway, I started down the street. I had pulled up to a stop sign when my cell phone rang. Hitting the speaker button, I said, "Hello."

"I should have eloped to Vegas." Amanda Beaumont's voice came through loud and clear.

"Ha!" I laughed as I continued to drive. "You're the one who wanted a glitzy wedding and fancy reception at the Marquette mansion."

"I swear," she said. "My mother will be the death of me. You're not going to believe what she's done now."

"What'd she do? Try and reschedule the bridal shower for the third time?"

"No," Amanda said. "It's worse."

"Meaning?"

"It's complicated."

"I'm on my way up to the mansion," I said. "It's move-in day. But if you want to get together tonight, Danielle is usually down by eight o'clock. We could meet up, have a couple of drinks, and I'm happy to listen to whatever is going on."

"Deal," Amanda said. "You are the perfect maid of honor."

"Well," I said, turning on to the cliff road. "I don't know about perfect, but after being a bridesmaid for Camilla, you are a *very* chill bride."

"You say that now..." Amanda groused. "Why don't you come over around 8:30 and I'll make that artichoke dip you like."

"The one with the little bread thingies?"

"Crostini," Amanda said. "Yes, that one."

"You had me at artichoke dip," I said.

"Thanks, Estella." Amanda laughed. "See you tonight."

I hit *end* and made my way up the steep hill to the mansion on the cliffs. After pulling into the entrance, I drove to the eastern wing of the big old manor house. Situated behind the mansion there was a converted coach house where Chauncey had a small apartment. I pulled beside the smaller building, taking an empty spot in the gravel parking area for the family.

I had barely shut the truck door when Chauncey came out to greet me.

"Hey, Aunt Lala," he said.

My shoulders automatically stiffened. The last thing

I had expected was for him to be there. He looked amazing as usual. Today he wore dress slacks and a casual, burgundy-colored *Trois Amis Winery* polo.

"Hey," I said, going for a casual tone of voice. "Your hair is different. Shorter."

He shrugged. "My stylist talked me into something different."

Stylist, I thought. *Sheesh.* I simply trimmed my hair myself, and he went to a stylist.

Suddenly I felt very underdressed in my t-shirt, faded jeans and sneakers. *Which is ridiculous,* I told myself. Tightening my ponytail, I marched to the tailgate of the truck and lowered it.

"Let me help you," he said, moving closer to take the suitcase.

"I've got it," I said, though he took it right out of my hands.

"It's no trouble," he said. "I promised Philippe I'd keep an eye out for you."

The man made me twitchy, and as usual, that pissed me off. I exhaled, told myself to stay frosty, and grabbed my duffle. Swinging it up over my shoulder, I shut the tailgate.

"Is this everything?" he asked.

I pocketed my keys. "Yeah, I know how to pack. My mother was military, remember?" I started around the side of the house toward the family entrance at the front.

Chauncey fell in step with me. "What about your

personal items?"

I slanted my eyes over. "Chauncey, not everyone has a thousand hair and skin care products like you do."

He stiffened. "That's not what I meant," he said.

I patted the duffle. "I have my soap, shampoo, conditioner and my makeup bag right here, in case you were concerned."

"I *meant* photos and mementos."

"That's not my style," I said, stepping onto the pavers at the family entrance area. "I travel light. Always have."

He hustled ahead of me to open the door. "Philippe took Danielle to the park so Gabriella could take a nap, and you would have the chance to settle in."

"Oh. Okay." I nodded.

"Philippe confided to me last night how relieved he is that you are staying with them for the next few months to help Gabriella."

I shrugged. "She's my sister. She needs my help, and I'm in a position to give it."

"You'll be sacrificing a lot of your personal life and free time," he said. "Have you thought about that?"

I stopped and considered him. "Not as much as *you* have apparently. You seem surprised that I would offer to help them."

He stayed where he was, and now I was caught between his arm and the door. "No, I'm not surprised. Damn it. I was trying to give you a compliment." He scowled down at me. "Do you have to always be so suspicious?"

I glared at him as he stood blocking my way. "You gonna let me in, Marquette, or are we going to stand here all day and argue?"

He muttered something under his breath but stepped back and allowed me to enter. I stopped and took in the lobby. The first floor of the eastern wing held Philippe's and the PR person, Nicole's, offices. There was also a restroom and a conference room.

Chauncey moved straight up to the wide wooden staircase that led to the upper floors of the eastern wing. He paused at the decorative shoulder-high wooden gate that sectioned off the landing on the second floor and entered in a code to unlatch it. The gate ensured that these floors stayed private, as they were for Gabriella and Philippe's family use.

Silently, we headed straight for the third floor where the bedrooms and the library were. At one section of the hall, I saw the heavy plastic barrier that had been erected to keep the construction dust to a minimum.

At the moment, Gabriella and Philippe had relocated to the guest room as they were expanding into the attic to make a new, more spacious primary suite. Once the renovations were finished, their original third-floor room would have a smaller footprint since they had given up part of the space to create a short hall and stairway to the new attic room.

I automatically went to the nursery. Chauncey opened the door and I glanced around at the soft aqua blue walls, lacy white curtains, and Cinderella theme décor. True to his word, Philippe had indeed set up a full-size bed and a small dresser. It was on the opposite side of the room from Danielle's toddler bed. The nursery was spacious, as it had been originally intended to hold several children at once, so there was more than enough room.

I tossed the duffle on the end of the bed and turned to take my other suitcase from him. Unfortunately, Chauncey stepped in closer at the same time that I reached for the case. We bounced off each other with the suitcase sandwiched between us.

I jumped back and he simply shut his eyes and shook his head. With exaggerated movements, he placed the suitcase on the foot of the bed. "Can I help you with anything else?" he asked politely.

"Nope," I said with forced cheer. "It will only take me a few minutes to unpack. No worries." So saying, I unzipped my duffle, opened a drawer, and started putting my things away.

"If you need anything, I'm working in my office for the rest of the afternoon."

"Okay, thanks," I said without looking at him.

He slipped out, and I waited a four-count, making sure he was gone before I lowered myself to the bed with a sigh.

When I'd offered to help my sister, it hadn't occurred to me that by living in the mansion with her family I would be in daily contact with Chauncey. But it should have, as he lived in the coach house and managed the hotel.

Two thirds of the mansion was a working hotel and event center. The hotel rooms were located on the western second and third floors, while the first floor held the ballroom, another reception area, the office area, and the museum room. Since Chauncey's office was in the western wing of the mansion, I hadn't realized I'd be seeing him that often. I had honestly assumed that he'd be busy all day.

I tried not to think about how he spent his nights.

I knew that he wasn't seeing anyone seriously at the moment, but considering his looks and how the dude used to hang out with supermodels and the Formula One race circuit, I didn't figure he spent many nights alone.

My attraction to him was an unfortunate circumstance, but after the past year, I'd had plenty of chances to practice ignoring it.

Most of the time.

You're doing it again, I warned myself.

"I have to stop obsessing over a man who doesn't see me as anything other than family," I muttered. I had to face facts: Chauncey considered me a friend at best...or a step up from the hired help at worst.

***

After peeking in on my sister who was sleeping in

the guest room across the hall, I tiptoed barefoot down to the second floor with plans to check and see what they had on hand for supper. However, the kitchen was a total disaster. Sippy cups and dishes were stacked in the sink. Plates and bowls were strewn across the counter. Gabriella took great pride in her home, and she'd be pissed to see things so messy.

As quietly as possible, I loaded everything in the dishwasher and scrubbed off the table and counters. Then I poked around to see what there was to cook with. In the fridge I found chicken breasts, chicken stock, fresh carrots, celery, and mushrooms, and a search through the freezer yielded frozen peas. Satisfied with my discoveries, I unearthed a big skillet. Adding olive oil, I heated up the pan and browned the chicken. Once that was done, I poured some stock into the skillet.

Quickly dicing up the carrots and celery, I dumped those in too. Normally I'd have added fresh onions, but considering Gabriella's nausea, I didn't think that'd be a good idea. Instead, I sprinkled in some milder dried minced onions and helped myself to the culinary herbs Gabriella had in pots in the windowsill. I added sage, thyme, and rosemary, tossed in some salt and a touch of pepper, and clicked the flame down to low and covered the dish.

Pulling dishes from the cabinets, I set the table while I was at it. I had just finished dicing the mushrooms when I heard Danielle's laughter from down the hall.

"Lala!" she shouted and ran to grab my knees.

"*Hola, mija.*" I picked her up and gave her a kiss on the cheek.

Philippe stopped at the entrance to the kitchen. "Are you cooking dinner?"

I tipped my head toward the big skillet on the stove. "Yeah, I'm making a sort of chicken vegetable stew."

"And you even cleaned the kitchen," he said. "I was going to do that tonight, but Danielle has been running me ragged today."

"Knowing Gabriella, she'd be upset to find her kitchen was trashed." I shrugged. "I figured it'd be best to clean everything up before she saw it."

"I didn't expect you to cook, Estella," Philippe said, "but I am beyond grateful for the help. I'm trying to get some sort of schedule set up for us."

"Drusilla said she'll bring by a few casseroles tomorrow for you to heat up."

Philippe pulled out a chair at the table and sat. "Camilla called me earlier and said she would be by with a few meals for us as well."

Poor guy, I thought. Philippe had to be stressed and scared. He'd been putting on a good show for Gabriella, but I could see that he was concerned. He looked exhausted. Hitching Danielle over to my hip, I added the mushrooms and the frozen peas to the skillet and stirred.

"This stew will make a lot," I told him, "so we can refrigerate any leftovers, and you can nuke some for lunch tomorrow."

"That's smart." He nodded. "If you don't mind keeping an eye on Danielle? I want to go up and check on Gabriella."

"Sure thing." I tucked the baby in her highchair, gave her a large plastic spoon, and she began banging away on the tray and jabbering to herself.

We managed ten minutes happily talking—well, I talked, and she babbled responses—before Chauncey strolled into the kitchen.

"Smells great in here," he said. "What's for supper?"

Instantly, my shoulders became tight. Determined to act casual, I sent him a smile. "A little something I conjured up."

He went over to the stove and lifted the lid. "It's not spicy, is it? I don't think Gabriella could handle that right now."

My smile evaporated. "Of course, it's not spicy! What am I, stupid?"

Chauncey shot me a look. "I simply wondered—"

"Wondered what?" I popped a hand on my hip. "That since I'm a Latina, everything I cook is probably made with jalapenos, cilantro, and chili powder?"

His eyes went huge. "Where did *that* come from?"

I sneered at him. "*Pendejo.*"

"I do not appreciate being called an asshole." Chauncey set the lid back on the skillet.

"Then stop acting like one," I shot back.

"Why is it I'm always taking grief from you?"

"Oh, I don't know..." I pressed a finger to my cheek as if thinking it over. "Maybe if you weren't acting so freaking superior all the time."

"You know, I'm damn tired of this routine. I try to be nice; you get prickly. I make a comment on the food, and you take it as an insult." In his annoyance his voice began to raise. "I walk in the room and your shoulders tighten. What did I ever do to you to deserve such a reaction?"

Danielle's face crumbled, and she began to fuss in her chair.

"There." I pointed at Danielle. "See what you did? You've upset the baby." I went over to Danielle, and as soon as I picked her up, the baby quieted.

"One of these days, Estella," Chauncey said, "you're going to have to stop hiding behind that nasty attitude."

"I'm not hiding behind it," I said. "It's a part of my charm."

Shutting his eyes, he sighed loud and long. "I have never been so tempted to throttle a woman in all my life."

"Ha!" I tossed my head. "I'd like to see you try, pretty boy. I'd have you eating the floorboards before you could blink."

"If you're going to make threats, you should put the baby down," he said. "Or are you merely bluffing?"

"Bluffing?" I shifted Danielle to my left hip. "You think you know me, Chauncey? I could drop you to your knees before you ever knew what hit you."

In response to my challenge, he stepped toward me. I pivoted so that Danielle was almost behind me, and at the same time I shot my right hand forward, palm facing out. It was a controlled thrust that I stopped a bare inch from his nose. Danielle squealed happily at the abrupt movement, and Chauncey's dark brown eyes almost bugged out of his head.

"Do *not* underestimate me," I said softly as he stared. "I have seen more, done more and defended myself in situations that would make you cringe." Slowly, I lowered my hand.

Chauncey took a deliberate step back. "Surely you know that I would *never* strike a woman." His voice was low, but his tone was serious.

"Lala!" Danielle bounced happily on my hip.

Before anything else was said, Philippe moved into the doorway

"Gabriella is awake." Philippe walked into the kitchen oblivious to the tension. "She said she would try and eat something in a bit."

"Good," I said, turning back to the stove as if to check the stew. "This should be finished in a few minutes. She can try some of the broth and the chicken and see how she tolerates it."

"Are you staying for dinner, Chauncey?" Philippe asked his brother.

"No." Chauncey's voice carried clearly to me. "I have dinner plans for tonight. Excuse me."

Of course, he has a date, I thought. Determined not

to let Philippe know that I'd almost decked his brother, I turned around from the stove with a smile in place and discovered that Chauncey had left. My shoulders dropped in relief.

Philippe took Danielle from me, and with a flourish and a bow, he pulled out a chair. "Mademoiselle."

I shook my head and sat. "Thanks, Philippe."

"Since you cooked," he said, tucking Danielle into her highchair, "I'm going to serve and clean up tonight."

"Deal," I said. "While you do KP, I'll take a bowl up to Gabriella."

"Perfect." He lifted the lid on the skillet and took an appreciative sniff. "This smells amazing."

I smiled at my brother-in-law, determined to put the altercation with Chauncey out of my mind. As Philippe dished up the stew and we began to eat, I had a moment to think how grateful I was that at least one of the Marquette brothers was charming and pleasant to be around.

CHAPTER THREE

Danielle was worn out by her trip to the park with her father and went down quickly. After having managed some broth, Gabriella had also fallen asleep and Philippe was sitting in the library with his laptop and answering emails. He assured me they were all fine and left the door to the hall open so if either Danielle woke or Gabriella called, he would hear them. I told him I'd be back later, gave him a quick wave, and headed over to Amanda's.

As usual, the back door of her old house opened for me before I could even knock. "*Gracias*," I murmured to the enchanted house. As soon as I walked in, I was hit with the aroma of baking. "Smells great in here," I said to my friend.

Amanda turned from the oven where she was pulling out the dip. "Hey Estella. How's Gabriella doing?"

"She's fairly miserable and stressed, but she stayed in bed and rested for most of the day. I think it helped some."

Amanda placed the artichoke dip on a trivet on her kitchen table. Immediately, my mouth began to water.

"It needs to cool off a bit before we eat it, unless you want to burn your mouth," she said, anticipating me.

I smirked at her friendly warning and saw that she was sliding tiny slices of French bread into her oven to toast. "You made the bread thingies. I can wait."

"Crostini," she said. "They're called crostini."

I pulled out a chair and made myself at home. "I call them delicious." Two plates, a bottle of wine, and wine glasses were already waiting on the table. Feeling at home, I poured a glass for myself and one for Amanda.

Amanda set the timer and joined me. "How did the move-in go?"

"Fine," I said. "I'm bunking in the nursery with Danielle for the time being. Philippe is pushing the contractor to hurry with the renovation to their new attic primary suite. He thinks they might be able to be finished in the next two weeks. Of course, they're keeping the news about the twins just to the family right now, but the contractor has seen Gabriella. It doesn't take a genius to figure out she's got some pretty bad morning sickness."

"How much is left for them to do?" Amanda asked.

"Philippe told me they were down to the finishes: tile in the bathroom, fixtures, paint, and touch ups. Once they have it all done, they'll have three bedrooms and two full bathrooms on the second floor. Which they are really going to need in the near future." I stopped and smiled. "I still can't believe they're having twins."

Amanda returned my smile. "I hope she'll feel better in time for the wedding."

"You've got almost seven weeks to go," I pointed out. "I think that most of the time, morning sickness eases up in the second trimester."

"Seven weeks may not be enough time for me to come to grips with the drama my mother has created."

"Your mom is so nice," I began. "What happened?"

"That's the problem," Amanda agreed. "My mother is nice and now she wants me to invite my sister to the wedding." The timer went off and Amanda rose.

"Wait." I blinked in shock at her announcement. "You have a sister?"

"I have two actually," she said. "Angela—she's twelve years younger than I am, and the baby of the family. She attends University in Florida."

"Florida is where your parents retired, right?"

"Correct," Amanda said, "but she's not the problem. It's my *other* sister. Her name is Arianna." Amanda deftly slid the toasted bread into a napkin-lined basket. "Arianna and I are not close. She has a checkered past, you might say."

"In all the time I've known you, neither you or your parents *ever* mentioned the fact that you have siblings."

"Part of that is because of our Guardian heritage," Amanda explained. "When my folks retired to Florida seven years ago, Angela was still in middle school. Dad had closed up some tough cases, and he wanted to keep

Angela off the local enemies' collective radars."

I nodded. "I understand."

Amanda exhaled. "My mom wanted a more 'normal' life for Angela, and after they moved, it simply became a habit not to mention my baby sister."

"So, Angela was in school when Vic and your mom came up to visit last year?"

"Yes," Amanda said, placing the bread on the table. "She was in her freshman year and stayed on campus. She's not a fan of Illinois and loves Florida. Besides, Angela thinks I'm simply a stuffy, boring librarian."

"I'd *never* call you boring." I chuckled. "You're a metaphysical bad-ass, Amanda."

Amanda fluffed her hair, making me grin. "Why, thank you," she said.

"Being the librarian is your day job *and* your cover for the Guardian post…in the same way that everyone in Ames Crossing thought your dad was merely a dispatcher for the sheriff's department. It's smart for you to blend in and fly under the radar. I get that."

"I didn't deliberately keep my sisters a secret from you, Estella," she said. "It was more of an automatic response."

"You don't owe me an apology, Amanda, but for what it's worth, I get why you kept your mouth shut. You were protecting your little sister." I took a sip of wine. "So, what's the story with the other one?"

"Arianna was another reason why my folks moved to Florida." Amanda sat beside me. "The gossip in the village was so bad about Arianna's reputation that it caused a strain on my parent's marriage."

"How *bad* are we talking?" I asked.

"Arianna had seduced an older man. A friend of the family. She was nineteen at the time, and he was forty. The affair destroyed his marriage and it also cost him his job."

"Holy crap."

"That's not the worst of it." Amanda grimaced. "She had no remorse over the affair. Arianna openly admitted to us that she'd seduced him, just to see if she could."

"Wow."

"Arianna also threw away her college scholarship, got into drugs, and was arrested for possession."

"She sounds like a real piece of work," I said.

"She managed to avoid jail, and then ran off with some guy to Arizona. She abandoned the family and wanted nothing to do with our Guardian heritage. We haven't heard from her in almost seven years."

"So why did she surface now?" I asked. "She want money or something?"

"My parents got a letter from her a month ago. She was asking to come and see them. Claims that she has her life turned around and wants to make amends."

I pushed a glass of wine toward my friend. "You don't believe her?

"No." Amanda took a sip of wine. "My mother says Arianna has changed, and that my sister has been clean for years now. My parents are very optimistic at the news...Anyway, they have invited her to come visit *and* to attend the wedding."

I paused in mid sip. "They didn't ask you first?"

"Nope. My mother spilled the beans last night." Amanda pinched the bridge of her nose. "Arianna will be arriving in mid-October, a week before the wedding. Mom thought maybe since the local B and B is full that Arianna could stay with me, here. In the house."

"Whoa," I said. "Are you serious?"

"We exchanged more than a few words over that." Amanda lifted her glass and gulped her wine.

"I'm sorry you had a fight with your parents."

Amanda set her glass down. "I told them under *no circumstances* would Arianna be staying with me. Nor would I be pressured into her being a wedding guest!"

"What did Zak say about all of this?"

"He was as blindsided as I was, but he agrees with me."

"Smart man."

"My parents foolishly believe she's changed. My father took my mother's side and started going on about how the wedding would be an opportunity to bring the family together again." Amanda adjusted her glasses. "I ended up shouting at them both. It was ugly, Estella."

"I'm so sorry," I said.

Amanda sighed and dished up some of the artichoke dip. "I never thought I'd have to worry about my prodigal sister's return upstaging me on my own wedding day."

"That's not going to happen," I said. "I'll see to it personally."

Amanda's lips curved slightly. "Estella Flores Midnight, no mere maid of honor...she also doubles as a security guard."

I nodded in agreement. "Nobody messes with my friend's special day."

Amanda added crostini to a plate and passed it over. "Arianna showing back up and somehow managing to make me into the villain, and herself the victim, was one contingency I hadn't planned on."

I happily accepted the plate. "Girlfriend, you are marrying a deputy. There will be officers from the sheriff's department all over the reception. *If* she attends, she wouldn't dare try anything funny, and if there's any drama...I'll knock the bitch unconscious and lock her up in a closet until the reception is over."

"Maybe you could do that *before* the ceremony and save me the stress?" Amanda asked hopefully.

I cracked my knuckles. "It'll be taken care of."

Amanda began to laugh. "Don't tease me."

"I'm dead serious," I said, scooping up some dip. "It's a big damn house. People get lost in it all the time."

"All I wanted was an elegant fall wedding. Quiet, classy and romantic." Amanda gulped her wine again. "Now, I have to deal with the fact that my parents think *I'm* selfish and unforgiving."

"People have to earn forgiveness," I said around a

mouthful. "Your sister is a fool to think she can just show up and have people roll out the red carpet for her."

"You don't understand," Amanda said, serving herself some of the dip. "Arianna is stunningly beautiful. People have always given in to her. She continuously finds a way to get whatever she wants."

"I promise you," I said. "Your sister won't be able to bullshit her way around me. I'm immune to the schmooze. Ask Chauncey."

Amanda paused before sampling the dip. "Uh-oh. Did you two get into it again?"

"It's nothing," I said. "But I do think we should do a deep dive into your evil sister's social media accounts. See what she's up to these days."

Amanda chuckled. "I had Leroy start an investigation into her recent activities last night."

"That's good." I pulled out my phone. "Spell her first name for me." It only took a moment, and I was looking at the woman's social media account. It was mostly New Age affirmations and goddess-theme quotes, with the occasional artsy selfie.

Amanda leaned over. "Yes, that's her."

Amanda's sister *was* beautiful. In the could-be-a-movie-star kind of way. She was a brunette, with clear blue eyes and a mane of long hair. "You know," I said, helping myself to more artichoke dip, "I have an automatic distrust of anyone who color coordinates their Instagram feed."

"It's too calculated," Amanda agreed. "There's no spontaneity."

"Yeah. I mean if you gotta work at it *that* hard, so everyone thinks your life is perfect, then you gotta be hiding something."

Amanda poured herself another glass of wine. "See? This is why we're friends. You are every bit as suspicious as I am."

"I have to admit, you having a renegade sister is a relief to me." I slanted her a look. "I was afraid when you said there was a wedding crisis, that you were going to tell me you'd changed your mind and I had to wear a hot pink bridesmaid dress."

"Gods no!" Amanda shuddered. "I battle evil for a living. I'd never subject you to the horrors of hot pink chiffon."

"I still can't believe I'm wearing tangerine," I mock-complained, nudging her with my elbow.

"You know the color is called *burnt orange*." She chuckled. "It was stunning on you, and as you are my only attendant, I wanted you to choose the fall color that best suited your dark hair and brown eyes, remember?"

"How could I forget? I tried on a half dozen dresses." I shuddered, dramatically. "The things I do for you."

She chuckled. "Have I mentioned lately how much your sacrifice was appreciated?"

I scooped up more artichoke dip. "The burnt orange

dress was the best color. Besides, it'll go great with all the pumpkins and fall leaves you're using."

"The final fitting for my bridal gown is in two weeks," Amanda said. "Did you want to come along?"

"I thought you were taking your mom..." I trailed off, as my friend frowned. "Sure, I can go."

"Thank you." Amanda heaved a sigh of relief. "I'm stressed enough without having to endure my mother going through the hard-sell as to why my sister should be a part of my wedding day. At the risk of sounding like a Bridezilla, I think my mother has forgotten that this is *my* special day, and not Arianna's."

"You're not a Bridezilla," I said firmly. "What you are is a woman a month and a half out from her big day, dealing with family bullshit that you totally don't deserve."

"Thank you, Estella."

Our conversation shifted to happier wedding things like the cake, the flowers, and the food. Though I could tell that Amanda was hurt by this wrench her mother had thrown into the mix.

Note to self, I thought. *At the first opportunity try and talk some sense into Amanda's mother.* Susan would lose her eldest daughter if she kept this up.

***

I soon settled into a sort of routine. I got up with Danielle in the morning, fed her and myself breakfast, and straightened up the kitchen afterward. Philippe tended to grab a cup of coffee and go, but he was right downstairs in his first-floor offices. I'd toss something in the crockpot for supper set the timer so the meal would be finished at 5:00, and go check on Gabriella to see if she needed anything. If she felt up to it, she'd sit with Danielle for a while.

On nice days I took the baby outside and let her run around. If it rained, we'd drop by Gran's or Dru's house and visit. Then we'd come back to the mansion, do lunch, and the baby would nap for a few hours. I'd toss in a load or two of laundry—jeez that kid went through clothes—and after she'd wake up, I'd try and keep her entertained until Philippe returned for supper.

Gabriella was having a rough time. It was hard to see her suffering so much. Even the special ginger lollipops that Gran had made for her during her first pregnancy weren't helping. She was seeing her doctor weekly and a visiting nurse came by twice a week. I thought maybe things were improving, and then she got worse. About two weeks after I'd moved in, Gabriella required another IV for dehydration, and this time, they admitted her to the hospital.

I received a text from Philippe, telling me that they were settled in a hospital room. I assured him that Danielle and I were fine, sent him a brief video of Danielle running around the gardens, and urged him to stay up at the hospital with Gabriella. Dutifully, I passed along the information in a group text to the family and told myself not to panic. My sister was in the best possible place for her and the babies. They were all receiving excellent care.

Unfortunately, my phone had been blowing up. Cammy kept bombarding me with texts demanding either more information or an update. She didn't want to disturb Gabriella or Philippe, but I was fair game apparently, and she was getting on my damn nerves.

Her constant texts were too distracting. I'd just answered her most recent request for more news—there was none—and I barely managed to stop the baby from eating a handful of dirt. She'd probably swallowed some of it, but I managed to get most of it out of her mouth. I was pretty sure anyway...

My phone rang again. Camilla was calling now, and suddenly, out of the corner of my eye, I saw that Danielle had shoved a handful of rocks in her mouth. I chucked my phone and lunged after her. The resulting toddler tantrum from being denied her "treat" was loud and long. After snaking a finger into her mouth to fish out any rocks, I got them. Then Danielle gagged, yelled, and promptly bit the crap out of me.

"Ow!" I yelled as she chomped down. Finally, I got her to let go and now had a perfect set of upper and lower teeth marks on my index finger.

Sensing freedom, Danielle made a break for it. I lunged forward, made a grab, picked her up, and tucked her under my arm as she kicked. "Girlfriend, you just went too far."

Danielle arched her back and fought for all she was worth.

"Knock it off," I told her and marched back towards the mansion. I scooped up my phone on the way and hauled a hysterical, angry toddler through the gardens around the house and all the way to the family entrance. "Look," I panted as I fought to open the main door. "I get that you know something is wrong." I managed to open it when suddenly Danielle flung herself backwards in a tantrum, almost whacking her head on the door jam.

Frightened at the narrow miss, I clamped down on her harder to better control her flailing about.

Nicole Dubois came running from her office. "Oh my," she said. "She's in a real temper today."

"Understatement," I said over Danielle's screeching.

Nicole helped me inside and shut the door. "She needs a time out, or a nap."

"A nap is right where we're headed."

"Good luck." Nicole gave me a wave and headed back to her office.

Danielle continued to cry and fight as we went up the stairs.

"*Mija*, I understand that you're mad, and that you want your mama," I said, unlocking the privacy gate, "but today and for the next few days it's you and me kid." I patted her back, hoping to settle her, and kicked the gate shut with my foot. "Let's calm down...it'll be okay."

In response, Danielle turned her head and bit my shoulder.

"Hey!" I gave her a light swat on her diapered butt to get her to let go. "Cut that out!"

It worked. She let go with her teeth and looked at me square in the eye. Her bottom lip poked out, began to tremble, and then the water works started. The toddler sobbed, with real tears, and I felt like the most horrible person in the world.

"*Madre de dios*," I muttered and hauled Danielle up to the third floor.

Taking her straight to the nursery, I pulled off her shoes and tossed them aside. I changed her diaper and she fought me the entire time. Grimly, I put her in bed. "You stay right there," I said, pointing at her.

Danielle flung her arm over her eyes.

"Yeah, yeah," I muttered, rubbing my shoulder. "At the moment, I don't like you either."

She let out a shuddering cry, and I took a light blanket from her bed and covered her up. "Here's your lovey." I handed her a favorite stuffed animal. "Now you chill out."

I walked to the doorway, switched off the light, and stood there watching her for a few moments. My phone continued to loudly buzz with incoming text messages. I made sure none of them were from Philippe, and then switched the phone to silent and tucked it back in my pocket.

Danielle lowered her arm to peek at me and twisted

away. Thankfully, she rolled over and promptly fell asleep. With a sigh of relief, I backed away from the door and went across the hall to the bathroom to wash my hands. Both my finger and shoulder were throbbing from where she'd bitten me.

My finger was turning purple, and my shoulder was red, but there was no broken skin. I had to give the kid points for fighting back hard, even if I hadn't deserved it.

I left the bathroom, made sure the nursery monitor was on, and saw that she was indeed out for the count. After securing a baby gate in the doorway of the nursery, I went down to the second-floor level to the kitchen.

God, I wanted a drink. But I was responsible for her. It wasn't exactly appropriate to start day drinking over a toddler's melt down.

I switched on the portable baby monitor's speaker on the kitchen counter, so I would hear if she woke up and started moving around. Opening the fridge, I settled for a soda. I popped the top of the aluminum can, dropped into a chair at the table, and prayed the caffeine would keep me going. My phone continued to vibrate, and I pulled it from my pocket and placed it on the table. As I watched, several more text messages from Camilla rolled across the screen.

I was wiped out from Danielle's tantrum and aggravated with my sister's non-stop texting. Ignoring the phone, I took a few precious moments to myself and sat there wondering what I could have done differently to have avoided such a meltdown of epic proportions from my niece.

"Note to self," I muttered. "Look up ways to avoid a toddler tantrum online."

The phone kept on vibrating. Now Camilla was calling. I let the call go to voice mail.

"Estella?" Chauncey's voice was low as he moved down the hall.

God damn it, I thought. *Exactly what I don't need.* "I'm in the kitchen," I answered, glancing over as he walked in.

It was obvious that he was worried. "Where's Danielle?" he asked.

"Passed out in her bed," I said. On the table my phone vibrated so much that it started sliding across the polished surface.

"Philippe sent me a text that Gabriella had been admitted," he said. "But I don't know much else."

"Gabriella has lost weight and was dehydrated," I said. "Her doctor is going to try a few things to see if they can help her. Philippe said something about electrolytes too..." I trailed off as the phone began to vibrate again.

CHAPTER FOUR

"Is that Philippe calling with news?" Chauncey asked.

I glanced at the phone. "No, it's Camilla, hounding me to death, wanting an update."

"Well, perhaps if you'd simply answer the phone, she'd stop calling."

"I've had my hands full here!" I snapped. "Danielle had a major meltdown in the gardens. She was eating rocks, I had to get them out of her mouth, and she bit the crap out of me. Then I had to haul her all the way up here while she's at DEFCON 1. She was fighting me so hard she almost whacked her head on the door jam! She ended up biting me again, and I swatted her butt, and put her to bed. Now I'm pretty sure that she hates me..."

"I see." Chauncey pulled out a chair and sat beside me. "That *is* a lot to handle."

I glared at him. "Don't you dare patronize me!"

"I'm not," Chauncey said. "I've seen that girl have a

tantrum. She's quite the handful."

My phone began vibrating once more. Seeing it was Camilla, I snatched up the phone and hit *accept*. "I swear to god, Camilla," I growled into the phone. "If you don't stop calling me every two minutes, I'm going to kick your ass from here to the state line!"

"She's *my* sister and I'm worried!" Camilla snapped back. "You wouldn't understand. I've loved her my whole life, and if you'd simply answer your damn phone I wouldn't have to keep—"

Furious, I cut her off. "I have NO more news. If I did, I would have told all of you immediately. What I *do* have is my hands full with a pissed off toddler who misses her parents, and in case you've forgotten, Gabriella is my sister too! I'm just as worried about her as you are!"

Fed up, I began to swear at her in Spanish, and Chauncey nipped the phone out of my hands.

"Camilla," he said. "Chauncey, here. Estella's had a rough afternoon with the baby. If we get any news, I will be sure to pass it along."

"And stop bombarding me with texts," I said loud enough so she would be able to hear.

Chauncey finished the call with assurances and a polite goodbye. Afterward, he gently placed the phone back on the table. "She's upset, Estella. Don't be so hard on her."

"Don't be so hard on *her*?" I blinked at him. "Apparently, I'm good enough to babysit in a pinch, but when push comes to shove, Camilla reminds me that Gabriella was her sister—and not mine. After a year of the Midnight family telling me that I was a part of them, at the first crisis I was put firmly in my place as a second-class citizen."

Chauncey rested his hand on my arm. "I'm sure she didn't mean it that way."

"Oh, I think she did." I pushed away from the table and grabbed the portable speaker. "I need some air," I said. "If I get any news, I will pass it along to you."

"I'm staying here, to help you with Danielle for the rest of the day."

"I don't need your help," I said firmly.

"Well, you've got it, nonetheless. I'll take care of dinner too."

"Fine." I jerked a shoulder. "Whatever."

I left him in the kitchen and went upstairs, letting myself out onto the third-floor balcony. The structure was made from the same stone as the rest of the big old house and offered amazing views of the cliffs and the river below. I stood at the ornate, chest high railing and stared out over the landscape, trying to get myself to settle down. The wind was brisk, and clouds were billowing up in the west. I studied the clouds boiling up in the sky and shook my head at how similar those threatening clouds were to my own feelings.

With a sigh, I could admit that Camilla's comment had cut me deeply. Mostly because it was so unexpected. She'd made me feel like an outsider again, and I was surprised at how badly that had hurt. I felt tears well up, and ruthlessly, I squashed them down.

Camilla lives her perfect life surrounded by relatives who adore her, I thought. *She's never known hunger, abuse, fear, or isolation. She's a spoiled princess, married to a doting husband and playing at being a mommy to her six-year-old stepson. What does she know about how hard it is to keep a strong-willed toddler entertained and safe every day?*

I winced at the nastiness of my own thoughts. Taking a deep breath, I blew it out slowly, trying to release some of the anger that I felt. A cry sounded over the baby monitor, so I squared my shoulders and went back inside to check on Danielle.

I ended up picking up Danielle and holding her for a few minutes. Chauncey appeared briefly in the doorway and I waved him off. The baby dropped her head to my shoulder and feeling exhausted myself, I stretched out on my bed and let her lay with her head pillowed on my chest. It had been a hell of a day.

She was upset and so was I. Maybe a bit of a cuddle would help her settle. I lay there rubbing her back until she fell asleep again. I ended up drifting off too and woke up with a start maybe an hour later to find Chauncey had come in to check on us.

He was smiling as he bent over me. It was a sweet, tender smile that had my belly clenching with longing. "Want me to put Danielle back in her bed?" he whispered.

He's only smiling at the baby, I told myself.

I nodded and he reached for her. Which meant his hands were going to be brushing against me as he picked up the baby. My heart slammed against my ribs, but his touch was brief and impersonal. He easily picked Danielle up and carried her across the room. Bending over, he laid her on the low toddler bed. With efficient moves, he covered her with the light blanket.

I had rolled to my feet while he'd settled the baby. My ponytail had slipped so I yanked the holder out of my hair and shoved the tie in my pocket. Stifling a yawn, I shook my head to try and wake up fully.

Chauncey had moved to the door and had the portable speaker in his hand. "Let's sit out on the balcony for a while," he said softly.

I nodded and went out, pausing to put the baby gate back up. Chauncey moved across the hall, opened the door to the balcony, and held it open for me. Once I was out, I lifted my face to the breeze and took a steadying breath. Truth was, I'd been too pissed off earlier to appreciate how pretty of a space Gabriella had created out here for her family.

The outdoor space was not only accessible from the hall, but also from the French doors off the former primary bedroom. Philippe had added sheets of Plexiglas in a wooden frame to the inside of the stone railing as soon as Danielle had started to crawl, making it safer, but the clear material did not obstruct the view.

There was a café table and chairs, and another duo of

comfortable outdoor chairs with a small table between them farther along the balcony. Lanterns flanking the second set of doors would add illumination at night. Several pots of fall flowers thrived on the terrace, and morning glories were scrambling up one side of the house.

After admiring the area, I went to the balcony and rested my elbows on the wide stone railing. Chauncey joined me. Facing the river, I watched as the sun dropped lower in the western sky. I managed maybe a minute and a half of peace before I remembered my cell phone. Worried that I may have missed a call from Philippe, I hurriedly checked.

There had been no new messages or missed calls from my brother-in-law, and mercifully none from Camilla. Flipping the silent mode to *off*, I shoved the phone back in my pocket.

I had only started to relax again when Chauncey placed his hand on my shoulder, and it made me jump almost a foot straight up in the air.

"I didn't mean to startle you," he said.

The wind chose that moment to blow all my hair into my eyes. After swiping at it, trying to get it out of my face, I gathered it up and twisted it into a rope over my shoulder. I kept my hand on my hair and decided my best move was to simply ignore my overreaction to his touch.

He continued to leave his hand on my shoulder. It took everything I had to stand there and act as if everything was normal. But the truth was, each time the man got close I started to sweat.

"In case no one has told you lately," he began, "what you're doing, helping out Gabriella and Philippe like this, is incredibly generous and kind."

I slanted my eyes over to his face. "Thank you," I said carefully.

He looked at me with the smallest of smiles hovering on his face. "And now that you've received a compliment, you're waiting for some sort of criticism."

"I only wanted to help them," I said. "My part-time jobs are of no consequence. I'm literally the poor half-sister the Midnights took in."

Chauncey turned to me. "You don't mean that."

"I came to this family party late," I reminded him. "The rest of them have their pretty lives to live. I sort of float along on the peripheral."

"I find it unbearably sad, that you consider yourself to be less."

I shrugged.

"Estella." He shifted his hand to cup the side of my face. "You are loved. Surely you know that."

"Maybe." In defense, I covered his hand with my own and gently pulled it away. "You may have noticed that I'm slow to trust."

"Why is that?" he asked, turning his hand so that now he held mine.

"Do you know what it is to be on your own?" I asked him. "Really alone, Chauncey, with absolutely no one to count on?"

"No," he said.

"Well, I do," I said. "I spent years scared, often hungry, and fighting to survive."

"I had no idea," he said. "No idea it was that bad."

"Except for Amanda, no one knows the details of my life after my mother passed," I said. "I haven't lied outright to the family, but I glossed over most of my life in California. Trying to make it sound like an adventure to Gran and Brooke..."

My words died when he gently cupped the other side of my face with his free hand. I simply stood there, dumbfounded, while he searched my eyes.

"Which explains," he said, "why you are such a capable fighter, and are often the first one to ride to the rescue or to offer help."

I reached up and captured his other hand. "I don't like hands close to my face."

"I'd never hurt you," he said, even as I drew that hand away too.

"It's instinctual with me. I'm not like the other women you've known," I tried to explain. "I've got scars and emotional baggage. I've done what I had to, to survive."

We stood face-to-face as he held both of my hands lightly in his. "I see," he said.

"Do you?" I held his gaze as I spoke so he would *finally* understand how different I was from the rest of the family. "I was taught controlled holds, and self defense moves from another bouncer because I had my ass handed to me a couple of times. I couldn't afford to go to a hospital, and I didn't want to be injured that badly ever again. So, I learned to take a punch *and* how to throw one."

"You took boxing lessons?" he asked.

"No." I shook my head. "No formal training, but I worked hard, and was taught by bouncers, ex military, and from a couple of bad-ass drag queens how to fight creatively with whatever is at hand."

"That should have never been necessary," Chauncey said.

"It absolutely was," I said. "Fighting dirty kept me from being beaten or raped. I've lived a hard life, Chauncey. It's made me tough and capable, but I'm no one's hero."

"I disagree. You are the most valiant woman I have ever known," Chauncey said, and then he leaned forward and kissed me.

His lips touched mine, and the kiss was soft and comforting. I held onto his hands for dear life, and my stomach promptly tied itself into knots. I was afraid to move, afraid to even breathe—I wasn't sure what his kiss actually meant.

Was this an 'I'm sorry' kiss, meant in comfort...or was it more?

He lifted his mouth from mine and gazed into my eyes. "Estella," he whispered and lowered his mouth to mine again.

This time the kiss was *more*, and I responded to it as I'd always wanted to. I let go of his hands, wrapped my arms around his neck, and pulled him closer to me. Our chests bumped and I opened my mouth to his.

Chauncey's tongue touched mine and I groaned. Now we were plastered all over each other. His hands were around my waist, and this was the kiss I'd waited a year for. Deep, wet, urgent, and hot as hell.

Our tongues dueled. He slid his hands slowly over my butt, and in response I bit at his lower lip.

Danielle's cry sounded from the baby monitor speaker and guiltily, we broke apart. I took one step back from him. "Danielle's awake," I said.

With his eyes locked on mine, Chauncey wiped his middle finger leisurely across his bottom lip. It was as if he was trying to capture the last bit of our kiss. The gesture was sexy as hell, and my knees almost buckled.

"I should go," I said. "She'll be hungry."

He tilted his head slightly to one side. "Go," he said, and his voice was low and husky.

With a nod, I went back inside the house and headed for the nursery.

"Oh my god," I breathed as I went to Danielle.

I'd kissed the crap out of Chauncey Marquette, and there was no coming back from that.

***

I wasn't sure what to expect when I brought Danielle

down to the kitchen for her supper. But to my surprise, Chauncey was standing at the stove and heating water for pasta. I spotted a jar of marinara sauce out on the counter and the makings for salads arranged neatly beside it.

I slipped the baby into her highchair, and Danielle slapped her hands on the tray and began to babble.

I was thrown for a loop when Chauncey cheerfully went about making supper, as if that brain-frying kiss hadn't just happened. Keeping a suspicious eye on him, I set the table. He chatted easily with me and made faces at the baby that she thought were absolutely hilarious.

Philippe walked in a few minutes later, and Danielle threw her hands into the air. "Dada!"

Philippe went immediately to pick up his daughter and give her a cuddle.

"How's Gabriella?" I asked him.

Philippe sat in a kitchen chair. "They are giving her fluids intravenously and medication for her nausea. She is very tired but feeling somewhat better. She threw me out of her room." He smiled. "Told me to go home and spend some time with Danielle."

"If she felt good enough to boss you around," I said, "then I would take that as a very good sign."

Philippe smiled. "They did another ultrasound to check on the babies. They looked good, had strong heartbeats."

"That's wonderful!" I said.

Philippe smiled. "They measured at the ten week and two days mark. It helped ease Gabriella's anxiety."

"And yours as well, I imagine," Chauncey said, dropping a hand on his brother's shoulder.

"I'm going to take Danielle up to visit her mother in the morning. That is, if Gabriella feels up to it," Philippe said.

"Good idea." I went to the counter and began making another salad. "You're right on time for supper. Chauncey's cooking." I stayed at the counter listening to the brothers talk. Once I finished, I plunked the salad bowls down on the table.

Philippe reached out and rested his hand on my wrist. "I appreciate everything that you're doing for us, Estella."

I slid my hand out from under his. "Hey, like I said. I'm happy to help."

"And thank you, Chauncey, for cooking tonight." Philippe smiled.

"It's not much." Chauncey shrugged. "But it'll do."

"How was Danielle this afternoon?" her father asked me.

"She ate dirt and tried to swallow rocks. Bit the crap out of me when I fished them out of her mouth…then she threw a tantrum and got put down for an early nap." I smiled. "She was fine."

Philippe started to laugh. "I will never understand this child's fascination with eating dirt."

"Maybe she takes after her Aunt Dru and will be a

gardener," I said, fetching the salad dressing from the fridge.

"She has her mother's stubbornness, for certain," Philippe chuckled.

Danielle rested her head against her father's chest and sent him a winning smile.

I placed the dressing on the table. "And she has her daddy's charm—when she decides that it suits her."

"She definitely has her Aunt Estella's fighting spirit," Chauncey said, dumping the pasta into a strainer.

Taken aback by the comment, I went back to the counter. "Smooth," I said under my breath, so only he would hear. While Danielle babbled away to her father, I popped open the lid to the marinara sauce and passed it over to Chauncey.

"I'll be right back." Philippe stood up. "Someone needs to be changed." He carried Danielle out and up the stairs to the nursery.

Chauncey slid the noodles back in the pot, and then poured the sauce over the pasta. "I want to see you, Estella," he said in a low voice.

"We've been seeing each other almost every day since I moved in the mansion," I pointed out. "You're seeing me now. In fact, I'm standing right next to you, *güey.*"

"Way?" he frowned.

"*Güey.*" I rolled my eyes. "It's slang. The word means dude."

"Regardless." He slanted me a look out of the corner of his eyes. "You know what I meant. I want to spend time with you."

My stomach clenched at his words. "Don't think that's possible," I murmured. "I'm on Danielle duty for the foreseeable future."

He stirred the pasta. "We can find a way. I want to be alone with you."

"Why?" I asked bluntly. "Why now?"

"I should think that would be obvious," Chauncey said.

"Oh." My stomach dropped in disappointment. "You want a casual hook-up. Is that it?'

He flinched. "*What*?"

I narrowed my eyes. "I've never been an easy lay, Chauncey."

He frowned. "I never said—"

"No, you didn't," I interrupted him. "You hadn't gotten that far yet."

"Estella!" He sounded shocked.

"You're not the first guy to assume that a girl like me would be grateful for a chance to have someone like you, pay attention to them."

With a scowl, he switched off the heat under the pot, and turned to dump the spaghetti into a serving bowl.

I took his silence for a confirmation. It was disappointing, but I should have known better. The bottom line with men was always to see how fast they could get in your pants. I knew that. I'd simply hoped that maybe Chauncey was different.

Above us on the third floor I heard Danielle laugh, and I started to reach for the serving bowl. "I can put that on the table for—"

The rest of my words were cut off as he spun around and laid one on me.

It was a scorching hot kiss. It never wavered as he walked me backwards until my hips hit the counter. Once we came to a stop, he slid his arms around my back and pulled me close. My brain promptly went to mush as he kissed whatever common sense I'd ever possessed right out of my mind.

Abruptly, he lifted his mouth. "Nothing about you is *easy*, Estella. I'm not looking for a hook-up, or casual sex. I am, however, interested in you." He kissed me again quickly and stepped back. "Philippe's coming down the stairs," he murmured.

I nodded once and moved to the side. When Philippe walked into the room, I was sitting in a kitchen chair, and Chauncey was transferring the bowl of pasta to the table.

Somehow, I got through the meal. Mostly because I kept my eyes either on my plate or on my niece. Danielle provided a good distraction as she flung spaghetti all over the highchair and the floor. I volunteered to give her a bath afterward. It was a good way to escape.

Because I needed to think very carefully about what Chauncey had said to me.

***

The dream was familiar—I'd experienced it before. I tossed and turned, trying to escape it, but it crashed over me with no remorse and absolutely no mercy...

Thunder was rumbling and lightning flashed in the distance as a man held me close, kissing me passionately. He pressed kisses to my face and hair swearing that he loved me. He told me he'd do anything, if it meant we could finally be together...and that he couldn't live without me.

But his declaration didn't feel loving or romantic because I was afraid. When he asked me to run away with him, I refused. It hurt me to do it, but I did. Terrified, I yanked away from him and then...I ran.

As fast and as far away as I could.

The storm broke, and the rain that fell mixed with my tears. I could barely see. My long skirts twisted around my legs and caused me to fall—hard. I pushed myself to my feet and continued on...even though my heart was breaking. All of my hopes and dreams were completely shattered, but I had to escape. I had to return home.

Still, he shouted after me.

Victoria, I love you!

His desperate voice woke me up.

CHAPTER FIVE

I sat straight up in my bed, sweaty and disoriented. I looked around and confirmed for myself that I was still in the nursery at the Marquette mansion and my niece slept across the room from me.

I knew that the dream was a brief window into the past, of my ancestor, Victoria Midnight, *and* of Chauncey's ancestor, Pierre-Michel Marquette. The star cross lovers had lived and died some one hundred and seventy years ago.

With a groan, I climbed out of bed in desperate need of some air. I tiptoed across the room in my oversized t-shirt that I'd slept in and went across the hall and to the doors that led to the balcony. As quietly as possible, I opened them and went outside. Overhead a waxing moon played peek-a-boo with passing clouds. I went to my favorite spot at the railing and leaned against it.

I stayed there enjoying the moonlight. The stone was cold and slightly damp, and it helped to ground me a little. I had only started to settle down from the nightmare, when, out of the corner of my eye. I saw the flicker of light. Yanking my head around, I discovered that I was no longer alone on the balcony.

The figure of a woman stood nearby, surrounded by light. Her long red hair spilled down and over the shoulders of an old-fashioned yellow dress.

"Victoria," I said. "Why are you here?"

Since Victoria Midnight's ghost had made her big visitation at Danielle's first birthday party six months ago, she'd been absent. We'd all figured that after she had announced to Amanda that she was *her* direct descendant—and not the evil Louisa Midnight's—that her spirit was now at rest. Clearly, we'd been wrong.

"Help us," the spirit said.

"Help who?" I asked.

Victoria clasped her hands together almost as if she were praying or begging. "Please, set him free."

I didn't need to ask who *him* was. Her lover, Pierre-Michele Marquette, had been forcibly bound to his portrait months ago. I'd been on hand to witness Amanda yank the spirit out of Chauncey—who he'd brutally possessed—and send Pierre-Michel's soul back into the old portrait.

"I don't know where Pierre-Michel is," I said.

"The Guardian knows," she said. "Go to Amanda. Ask her to set him free."

"I can't do that," I said. "The last time your boyfriend was loose he possessed Chauncey. He hurt him. I won't let that happen again."

"You will change your mind," Victoria practically growled. "You must!"

I was shocked at the change in the ghost's demeanor. *Could ghosts even have a demeanor?* I wondered.

"You have no choice!" she insisted. "Set him free!"

I shook my head. "No, I won't."

Suddenly she was up in my face and her hands clamped down around my upper arms. "I will *make* you."

"Back the hell off," I said, as I found myself trapped against the railing. I struggled against the ghost, but no self-defense moves could work against an incorporeal being. There was nothing physical for me to grip, strike, or to throw my weight against.

She bore down on me. "Release him!"

"Stop it!" I demanded, feeling the stone railing cut into my back.

Caught between the ghost and the rail, I strained against the supernatural force that bent me backwards. I was battling against something that shouldn't have been possible, and yet I felt her grip tighten. The railing was high. I didn't think she could push me over, but still; I had a few seconds of gut-wrenching fear. A fall from this height would be deadly.

"Victoria Midnight." I spat the words out, as beneath my shoulder blades the stone railing ground deeper into my skin. "I banish you!"

"No, you will not." She pushed even closer, leaning down into my face. "I have walked these grounds for over a hundred and seventy years waiting for my love." Her lips peeled back from her face, and the sheer force of her anger was suffocating. "You have no power over me, lost star."

"Victoria Midnight," I whispered, gasping for breath. "I banish you."

With a snarl, she pressed closer, and her face was terrible to look upon.

My hands scrabbled for purchase but there was nothing to grip. One hand brushed against the stone wall of the house, and I felt the morning glory vines. A tiny bit of magick zinged through me. Blindly, I grasped for the flowering vines. They seemed to wrap themselves around my fingers, almost as if they were trying to help me.

"Victoria Midnight," I tried to speak again, but it barely made any sound. Gritting my teeth, I pulled up my power from the gut. Amanda had taught me that without intention, magick was nothing, and so I fixed my will towards banishing the threatening spirit.

I banish you! I mouthed the words and put all my intention behind it...and suddenly she was gone.

Now free from her attack, I fell forward, landing hard on my hands and knees.

Coughing, I drew in a deep breath. Then another. My head was spinning, and my heart was pounding so hard that I was afraid I might pass out. It had felt like I'd been drowning.

In my fall I had yanked some of the morning glory

vines free. They remained wrapped around my wrist in a sort of bracelet. I left them as they were, and as soon as I was able, I pulled myself to my feet and got the hell off the balcony.

Shutting the doors, I locked them with shaking hands. The hallway was quiet and more importantly it *felt* normal. Still, I immediately went and checked on the family. Philippe was out cold, and Gabriella's cat, Shadow, was curled at the foot of the bed. The cat glared at me, and I left his bedroom door open a few inches and raced to the nursery.

My niece was sitting up in bed looking confused. "Lala," she said.

I scooped her into my arms and took her to bed with me. I settled against the headboard, sat up, and the baby snuggled in deeper and went right back to sleep.

I brushed the hair back from Danielle's face and noted that from my vantage point on the bed, that I could see the foot of Philippe's bed. Satisfied with that, I tucked a pillow under my arm to help support Danielle's weight and prepared to keep watch over them both for the rest of the night.

***

The next morning, I discovered that the morning glory vines were blooming around my wrist. Baffled by it, I gently peeled them off, and tucked the vines and deep blue flowers under my pillow. I wasn't even sure why I did it...but my instincts insisted that I should.

I said nothing about my encounter with the ghost. Instead, I acted as if everything was fine, sending Philippe and Danielle off with a smile on my face. I stood waving from the lobby entrance, and as soon as I was sure they were gone, I pulled my cell phone from my pocket and called Amanda.

"First off," I said into the phone, "thank you for teaching me defensive magick."

"What's happened?" Amanda demanded.

"There's been another manifestation at the mansion, and I'm gonna need your help."

"Are you all right?"

"Kind of," I said. "It'd probably be better if I showed you."

Fifteen minutes later, I stood in Amanda's kitchen in my bra and jeans, with my hair clipped on top of my head, while she assessed the injury to my back and the bruises on my upper arms.

Amanda hissed out a breath. "Damn it, Estella! Those are serious bruises and a nasty looking scrape. You should have called me last night."

"Yeah well, at the time I was more concerned with making sure that Philippe and Danielle were both safe."

"Did the manifestation wake the baby?" Amanda asked.

"Not sure," I said, twisting the t-shirt that I held in my hands. "Philippe slept through it, but Danielle was sitting up when I rushed back to the nursery. I guess I woke her up when I shut the doors to the terrace."

"I doubt it," Amanda said. "Children are often more sensitive to the paranormal than adults. She probably knew something was wrong."

"She was fine earlier this morning. Philippe took her up to the hospital to visit Gabriella."

"That's good," Amanda said, patting my shoulder.

"I didn't say anything to Philippe about the ghost. The guy deserves to have a quiet morning with his daughter."

"Hmm." Amanda traced a finger over my bruises. "You have perfect fingerprint marks around your arms. That's never good when a spirit manages to do physical damage to a mortal form."

"A gift from Victoria to *my* mortal form," I said, with a sigh. "It totally creeped me out this morning seeing them. Then there was the blue morning glories, but that was sort of nice actually."

"Blue morning glories?" she asked.

Briefly, I explained. "It's probably just a coincidence," I said. "Dru would know. She's the gardener and plant magick expert."

"Mm hmm." Amanda nodded. "I have something I want to put on your skin. Not only for the physical wounds, but for the astral injuries as well."

"Astral injuries?" I raised my eyebrows. "Do you mean like that time you got sick from your exposure to that spirit at the antique store?"

"Exactly," she said. "Have a seat, I'll be right back."

"Okay." I tossed my t-shirt on the table. Turning a high-backed chair around, I straddled it so I could cross my arms up on the back of the kitchen chair. Tiredly, I dropped my head to my folded arms. The truth was, not only was I sore, but wiped out from using defensive magick; and because I'd sat up watching over Philippe and the baby all night long.

Nyx strolled into the kitchen, meowed when she saw me, and hopped right on the chair, squeezing herself between my chest and the chair back.

"It was a hell of a night, Nyx," I said, while the cat purred and burrowed close.

"Hey, Mandy." The kitchen door swung open and Leroy, Amanda's paranormal investigation technical guru and ghost hunting sidekick, waltzed right in, toting his ever-present equipment bag.

Belatedly, I picked up my shirt. Not that I was embarrassed to be sitting in my bra and jeans, but it was more out of courtesy. The man was old enough to be my grandfather.

"What in the sweet hell happened to you?" Leroy demanded, rushing closer.

"Tangled with a whacked-out ghost last night up at the mansion," I said, draping the shirt over my chest. "She tried to push me over a stone railing."

"Don't worry about covering up," he said. "I've seen a bra before, Dollface."

I scowled at him. "Don't call me 'Dollface.'"

He patted the top of my head and pulled up a chair

next to me. "I like calling you *Dollface*. It suits you."

"Listen, *anciano...*"

Leroy chuckled and set his bag on the table. "Ha! I looked that word up. You called me 'old man.'"

"You're lucky that's all I called you."

"Those are some mean looking bruises." He hesitantly touched a finger to my upper arm over the finger marks.

I flinched slightly at the touch. "It hurts."

Amanda came back into the kitchen. "Hi, Leroy," she said, apparently unsurprised that he dropped by.

He hooked a thumb in my direction. "Looks like your apprentice got her ass handed to her."

"I did *not* have my ass handed to me!" I insisted, even though I was secretly pleased to be called her apprentice. Amanda was a total badass in the magick department.

"Mm hmm." Leroy smiled and nodded pleasantly. "Have you seen what your back looks like, Dollface?"

"Sort of." Refolding my arms, I rested them on the back of the chair. "I saw my upper arms and a little of my back in the bathroom mirror at the mansion. It's hard to get a close look at it all though, considering where it's at."

"Have you documented her injury?" Leroy spoke to Amanda. "Bearing in mind everything that has happened up at the mansion, we should."

"I agree," Amanda said, "and I was going to."

"I'll do it," Leroy said and rose to his feet. He pulled

a camera from his bag. "I'm going to take a couple of pictures of the marks on your arms and back."

I'd been about to complain that it wasn't necessary, but I glanced over at Amanda. Her expression was set. "Okay," I sighed.

"Won't hurt a bit," he said cheerfully, and shortly thereafter I heard him snapping away with his camera.

I pulled my phone from the pocket of my jeans and handed it over my shoulder to him. "Take a few for me too."

"Will do," he said, taking the phone from my hand. A few moments later he passed the phone back.

I pulled up the images and my stomach rolled at what I saw. The handprint bruises were fairly clear and stood out on my skin. My back however was much worse. A wide scrape ran horizontally under my shoulder blades, surrounded by a large, dark purple bruise. Seeing it so clearly made it hurt worse somehow.

"Bat shit crazy old ghost," I muttered. "What made her snap and go from being all nice and comforting with Amanda, to acting mean and aggressive with me?"

"Tell me everything that happened last night," Leroy said, rooting through his equipment. "I'm going to record this and make notes later." He slid a small recorder across the table. "Okay with you?"

"Sure." Biting back another sigh, I put away my phone and quickly retold my experiences for Leroy. Once I was finished, Amanda started to work on my injuries.

"Put your arms back up on the top of the chair," she suggested. "Try and relax. This will sting."

I braced myself but jolted at the sting anyway. The salve she applied burned like crazy. "Damn it." I hissed a breath out between my teeth as she kept working. "It *does* sting."

"Hang on," Amanda said.

I steeled myself and dropped my chin down to my arms. "Just get it done."

The lights in the kitchen pulsed brighter. "Incoming," Leroy said to Amanda.

"What do you mean?" I lifted my head. "Incoming *what*?"

The kitchen door swung open and to my utter shock, Chauncey walked in. He was all slick and professional in a gorgeous dark suit, but he stopped dead, taking in the scene. I'm sure it looked beyond crazy. There I was straddling the chair without my shirt on. Amanda was behind me, working on my back, and Leroy sat beside me, with his camera and recorder out on the table.

"What are *you* doing here?" I asked.

"What happened to Estella?" he demanded at the same time.

"Thank you for coming," Amanda said to Chauncey.

I whipped my head around. "You invited him?"

Amanda gave me a hard look. "I did."

"I was in the village," Chauncey said, moving around me to see my back for himself. "That's how I was able to get here so quickly..." his voice trailed off.

I told myself not to be embarrassed. After all, I was more covered up than if I'd been wearing a swimsuit.

"Ghastly, isn't it?" Amanda asked him.

"Jesus, Estella!" Chauncey's voice was clearly horrified. "You should have called me last night."

"That's *exactly* what I told her," Amanda said.

"Listen," I began, "I told Amanda earlier, and now I'm telling you—" I flinched as Amanda applied more of the salve to the scrape. Pissed off, tired and in pain, I began to swear. "*Shit!*"

"Brace yourself, Dollface," Leroy said cheerfully. "It'll get a lot worse before it gets better."

"*Hijo de puta!*" I yelled as the salve she applied across my back went from an annoying burn across my flesh, to an intensely painful throb.

"What's happening?" Chauncey asked.

"Healing magick hurts," Leroy said, matter-of-factly.

Amanda began to chant. Her voice was quiet and calm, and I heard it clearly even as I swore in Spanish until I ran out of curse words.

I felt my eyes droop and my head nodded. With an effort I jerked my head back up. "Are you messing with my head, Amanda?"

"Take a nap, Estella," Amanda's voice sounded amplified.

"No." I yawned. "I'm not tired."

"Take a nap, anyway," she said, and then I was out.

***

I opened my eyes and discovered I was lying on my belly on Amanda's pretty navy-blue sofa. Her house was quiet and calm. I blinked a few times and discovered that while my back was still sore, the pain had faded to a milder ache. Slowly, I pushed up to my elbows and jolted when I saw Chauncey sitting in an arm chair a few feet away.

"How do you feel?" he asked.

I ran my tongue over my teeth. "Sort of woozy, but better."

I began to shift to a sitting position and was surprised when he jumped up to help me. Once I was upright, he silently handed me my shirt that had been folded and lying on the coffee table.

I accepted the shirt and glanced down at my arms. The bruises had significantly faded. "Well, damn," I said. "That's impressive."

"Do you need help putting your shirt back on?" he asked politely.

I scowled at him. "I think I can handle it." I tugged the shirt over my head, and slowly worked my arms through the short sleeves one at a time. I felt a good twinge when I pulled the shirt down my back, but honestly, I'd suffered much worse injuries.

He stood before me with a grim look on his face. "Amanda and Leroy filled me in on the events of last night."

"Okay, cool." I nodded. "Saves me the trouble."

"Don't brush this off, Estella," he said. "You fought for your life last night against a ghost who tried to force you over a third-floor balcony!"

"Yes, I know," I said evenly. "I was there."

"This changes things. We have to speak to—"

"No, we don't!" I interrupted him. "I don't want you to tell Philippe and Gabriella about any of this. They have enough going on."

He tossed his hands up in the air. "Are you crazy?"

"When Gabriella comes home, she'll need to rest and relax. She won't be able to do that if she's scared and or worried about—"

"You're right," he said, cutting *me* off mid-rant.

"You agreed with me." I blew out a long breath. "Damn it, you must be worried."

Chauncey sat beside me on the couch. "What do we do now?"

I pulled the clip from my hair. "For starters, I'll help Amanda conjure up some fresh ghost repellant charms, and I'll wear my Fifth Pentacle of Mars talisman again." With a sigh, I scrubbed my hand over my head. "I got lazy and forgot to wear it all the time. But I won't make that mistake again."

"No, you won't," Amanda said, walking into the room.

"I packed the talisman in with my things," I said to her. "I'll put it on as soon as I get back to the mansion."

Chauncey rested his hand on my arm. "I'm not

comfortable with you being in the mansion alone, Estella."

I rolled my eyes. "I'm never alone in that place. Besides the family, there are construction guys in the attic. Nicole works in her Public Relations office on the first floor, and you and all the hotel staff are over in the western two-thirds of the house."

"You know what I mean," he said. "I don't think that you are safe in the family wing."

Amanda spoke up. "Estella, I will come along with you to the mansion today. We'll ward all of the family's rooms, the bedrooms, and especially that balcony. Leroy has loaned you an EMF sensor. He has it calibrated to sound an alarm if the levels become elevated—"

"Which would let me know if a spirit was near," I finished for her. "I'm down with that."

"Will warding the family wing actually help?" Chauncey asked.

I scowled at him. "You're seriously questioning the woman who yanked a possessing spirit out of your body, re-bound it into a portrait, and then healed you— if she can manage to ward the house?"

"Magick is new to me," Chauncey said. "I've witnessed it, but I do not pretend to understand its intricacies."

Mollified at his answer, I shut up.

"Chauncey," Amanda said, "trust me to take care of this for your family."

"Our family," he corrected.

Amanda inclined her head. "I'm still getting used to the fact that all my father's ancestors and my own last name should have been Marquette and not Beaumont."

"Beaumont or Marquette we are family." Chauncey smiled. "But I'll leave this in your capable hands, Amanda. You're the expert."

"If you have no objections, I'd like to ward your residence as well," Amanda said to him.

"Of course," Chauncey said, checking his watch. "Unfortunately, I have a staff meeting at the hotel in fifteen minutes. I have to go."

I waved him off. "So, go. We got this."

He leaned over and planted a soft, lingering kiss on my mouth. "Be safe," he said, after lifting his mouth from mine. "I'll check in with you later."

Shocked that he'd done that, I sat there silently. Chauncey stood, said his goodbyes to Amanda, and let himself out.

The kitchen door closed behind him. Nyx jumped up to the couch to sit beside me, and eventually I shifted my eyes over to my friend where she stood peering over the top of her glasses at me.

"What?" I asked her. "You look like you're going to lecture me for being too loud in your library."

"What do you mean, *what*?" Amanda folded her arms. "Since when did you and Chauncey Marquette become an item?"

"*Madre de dios*," I grumbled. "We are *not* an item."

"That kiss says otherwise."

"I..." I lifted my hands and let them fall into my lap. "It's complicated."

"I'll tell you what's complicated," Amanda said. "My cousins are macking on each other, in my house."

"Hey! Chauncey and I are *not* related." I sat up straighter. "And did you really use the term, *macking*? You get in a new urban dictionary up at the library or something, Amanda?"

"No, we did not, but thanks to Pierre-Michele and Victoria Midnight you are both related to *me*, cousin." Her lips twitched. "And that was more than a casual kiss he planted on you."

"It was sneaky is what it was."

Amanda narrowed her eyes. "Normally I'd bombard you with questions. The only reason I'm not, is because you're recovering from a psychic attack, *and* we also need to get up to the mansion and get—"

"That's two reasons," I pointed out, interrupting her.

"—to work," she finished.

"I'm fine," I told her. "Let's get to it."

"I put together a few things while you were napping," she said. "I'm ready whenever—"

"I'm ready now."

"I may have mentioned this to you before," Amanda said, "but you have a very annoying habit of finishing people's sentences."

I shrugged. "Sorry."

Amanda snickered. "No, you're not."

I stood. "Let's go bust some—"

"Heads." Amanda spoke right over me. "In a spiritual sense of course."

"Nice!" I chuckled. "Excellent use of a Ghostbusters movie quote!"

Amanda tossed her dark red hair over one shoulder. "A girl does what she can."

CHAPTER SIX

Amanda and I warded the crap out of the family wing. We used salt water, incense smoke and magick to bind the area and make it impenetrable to ghosts. I added black tourmaline—that I charged with protective energies—to each room, making sure to place the chunks of crystals both out of sight and high up enough where Danielle couldn't get ahold of them.

I also recharged my talisman before putting it back on. It did make me feel more secure, with it lying firmly against my chest. I also got crafty and drew protective symbols and Runes with chalk under the baby's bed, my bed, and under Gabriella and Philippe's bed, too. Lastly, I scooted up the new stairs to the almost complete primary suite and added more protective symbols and Runes to that room as well.

We were finishing the clearing, cleansing, and blessing of the space, when Philippe and Danielle returned to the mansion. I took the toddler off her father's hands so he could try to get some work in for a few hours, and Amanda ducked out and headed over to Chauncey's apartment above the old coach house and did the same for his place. It seemed to work. For the next few days there were, thankfully, no other ghostly incidents.

Gabriella had improved enough that she was finally able to come home. While she'd been away there'd been a big push and the new primary suite had been completed. Gran came up to help hang curtains. Max and Nicole Dubois arrived and Nicole stayed in the nursery with their son Caleb and Danielle. She kept the children entertained and out of the way, while Chauncey and Max helped Philippe haul the furniture up the stairs.

I had to laugh over their swearing as they hauled everything up. The three men debated the furniture placement, trying to match Gabriella's original plan, until Gran stepped in. She took the plans and directed the three of them around.

As for me, I cleaned any remaining construction dust out of the new room and from the third-floor hallway. Pulling the linens, towels, and accessories for the new suite that Gabriella had set aside, I hauled everything upstairs. I hung up the towels in the bathroom and did my best to make the fancy spa-like space look pretty.

Gran seemed to think I'd done a good job. She and I made the bed so that when Gabriella was released from the hospital, she could go right up to her new room. Gran had even brought a vase of fall flowers from the farm and put them on the bedroom dresser. Once it was all finished, I had to admit the attic conversion was like something from a home improvement show. Hopefully it would cheer up my sister to come home to find the renovations all finished.

With a flourish, Philippe carried her up to their new attic suite and I followed with Danielle. Gabriella cried happy tears when she saw the finished room, and I passed the baby to her mother and excused myself so the three of them could have some time to settle in.

Drusilla and Camilla dropped by together a few hours later, and I decided to stay clear of Camilla. I still wasn't over that comment she'd made about how Gabriella was *her* sister. I used the unoriginal excuse of taking Danielle outside to the gardens and ducked out of their way, allowing the three sisters to have their visit in private.

Now Danielle ran across the grounds chasing a butterfly, and I sat on the grass and kept watch. In the distance, the mansion loomed, looking gothic and creepy. I blew out a long breath and told myself to let the anger go. I'd helped to make sure the old house was currently ghost free. Gabriella would now be safe to recover and raise her family there.

My shoulders tightened reflexively, and I knew we were no longer alone in the gardens.

"Cee-Cee!" Danielle shouted.

I tossed a look over my shoulder to discover Chauncey walking up the garden path. The first time he and I had met had been in this garden, the night before Drusilla's wedding. It'd been over a year ago and still, seeing him walk toward me had my heart slamming against my ribs.

I managed a casual smile. "Hey," I said.

Danielle made a beeline for him, and he scooped her up. "How's Gabriella settling in?" he asked me.

"Fine," I said, hooking a thumb over my shoulder. "Dru and Camilla are visiting with her right now."

He pressed a loud smacking kiss to Danielle's cheek, making her giggle. He set her back on her feet and she took off again. "May I ask why you are here in the gardens instead of up there with your sisters?"

I shrugged. "Just staying out of the way."

He sat beside me on the lawn.

"You're gonna mess up those fancy slacks sitting on the grass."

"I'm not worried," he said.

I smirked. "Bet your dry-cleaning bills are crazy high."

"Stop fussing, Mum."

I raised my eyebrows at that comment.

He grinned and took my hand. "Now that Gabriella's home and settling in, why don't you and I go out to dinner?"

"Well, I—Danielle, no!" I jumped up to grab Danielle before she decided to sample the gravel on the path again. Stuffing her under my arm I carried the toddler back to him. "Probably better ask Philippe if that's okay, first."

Chauncey reached for Danielle. "I already have." He settled the toddler on his lap. "Philippe is having a meal delivered tonight. It'd be nice to give the family a little privacy and quiet after the past few days."

I folded my arms. "It would be a treat to have supper without dodging food thrown by an eighteen-month-old," I said. "Where'd you want to go?"

"It's a surprise," he said.

I rolled my eyes. "Okay, but what sort of vibe are we talking? Casual like a burger joint, a diner that's come as you are, or a fancy place where I need to wear a dress?"

Chauncey climbed to his feet. "Casual would be best."

"I can handle that," I told him.

"Let's walk back together. I'll drop you and Danielle off and come back and pick you up in an hour."

I had barely enough time to throw myself into the shower and get date-ready for Chauncey. He'd said casual clothes, so I took him at his word and put on my new dark jeans, and after a bit of debate, I tugged a thin red sweater over my head. For shoes I had three options: sneakers, my one pair of dressy black heels, or my trusty short black boots.

"Boots it is," I said.

Pulling a black sharpie out of my drawer, I touched up the scuff marks on the toes and heels. I needed to replace the boots, but I couldn't afford to. Especially as

I wasn't bringing in a paycheck at the moment. The boots would be fine for now. Taking a critical look at the mending, I nodded in satisfaction. I put the pen away and fluffed up my hair. The only thing left was to tackle my face.

Squaring my shoulders, I grabbed my makeup bag and headed for the hall bathroom. I was applying my eyeliner when I recognized that my hands were shaking.

"Stop that." I scowled at myself in the mirror. My brown eyes were a little too wide, and my cheeks were flushed. Deliberately, I took a calming breath and leaned against the bathroom counter for a moment to steady myself. "You've waited a year, and you can handle him. Girl, you got this." With determination, I grabbed a tissue and wiped away the shaky eyeliner and began again.

I was finishing my second attempt at eyeliner when Danielle came barreling into the bathroom and grabbed ahold of my legs.

"Lala!" she giggled.

"Sorry." Philippe was moments behind her and scooped her up. "She got away from me."

"No worries," I said.

"You look nice tonight," Philippe said.

"Tonight?" I narrowed my eyes at his reflection in the mirror. "As opposed to how I typically look?"

He grinned. "If I've learned anything from being married to your sister, it's that when a daughter of

Midnight uses *that* tone, to be wary."

"Smart man." I selected a copper eye shadow and applied it to my lids. "Which is probably why she still keeps you around."

"Well, that, and Gabriella *worships* me."

Casting my eyes over to check his expression, I discovered he was laughing at his own glib reply.

He bounced Danielle on his hip. "Have fun tonight."

"Thanks. Do I have a curfew, Dad?" I asked tartly.

Philippe laughed and gave my hair a brotherly tug. He left, taking Danielle with him.

I was surprised when Chauncey picked me up, that instead of pulling onto the River Road and heading toward Alton, he drove his car into the village instead. We cruised slowly along the street, almost as if we were going to Amanda's. In fact, I could see her house.

"Where are we going?" I asked.

"You'll see." He smiled and pulled his car into the gravel driveway of an old two-story stone house. He slowly drove around the side of the home and I saw that the building kept on going. Jutting off the back of the old house was a more modern addition covered in gray siding. It featured a double car garage and a side door flanked by small windows trimmed in white. On the second floor above the garage, there was a trio of windows.

He parked in front of the garage doors, turned off the ignition, and smiled over at me.

"What is this?" I asked.

"A property that I've been looking at," he explained. "I'd like your opinion on it."

"My opinion?" I frowned at him. "I don't know anything about real estate."

"Be honest, and give me your first impressions," he said and climbed from the car. "Come on."

I pushed the passenger door open and followed him. To my amazement, he pulled a key from his pocket and opened the side door.

While he finagled the lock, I glanced around. "There's a fair amount of space between this house and the nearest neighbor—which is Amanda."

"Yes," he said, turning the door handle. "She's the one who tipped me off that the home had gone up for sale."

"I didn't realize you were looking for a house."

"I can't live in that tiny apartment above the coach house forever." He held the door open, and I went inside.

"Place isn't haunted, is it?" I asked, making him laugh.

"No," he said. "Amanda also assured me there were no significant metaphysical anomalies connected to the property's history either."

I shook my head. "If anyone else would have said that to me, I'd have thought they were crazy."

Chauncey shrugged. "When in Ames Crossing..."

"You've got a point."

We poked around the empty house. It was clean,

although it smelled stale as if it had been closed up for a long time. The kitchen was large, but the appliances were in desperate need of an update.

"The cabinets are solid and sturdy." I opened a cabinet. "Bet you could jazz these up with a coat of paint."

"That's what I thought," he said. "I might replace them. We'll see."

I walked across the kitchen, opened a door at random, and found a basement. I nodded and continued listening as Chauncey talked about the history of the original building.

"The stone house was built in 1858..." he began.

"Almost a decade after the big drama with Victoria, Pierre-Michel and of course his missing bride, Bridgette Ames," I interjected.

"Right," he said. "I'm happy there's no links to any of that. Anyway, the property has five bedrooms and 3 baths. The garage and floor above it were added in 1985, and on the other side of the addition there is a brick patio."

We walked around the lower level. I went one way while he stayed, continuing to poke around in the kitchen. The rooms in the original structure were nice, with hardwood floors and basic ivory walls. To my eye all they needed was a good scrubbing, new curtains, and fresh coat of paint.

I stuck my head into a room and discovered a downstairs bathroom. I cringed at the tacky decor and then grinned at my reflection in the mirror. Taking a deep breath, I let out a loud, hopefully terrified sounding scream.

Chauncey came running.

"*Madre de dios!*" I staggered back dramatically, my hands shielding my face.

"What?" he demanded.

"That's the most hideous wallpaper I've ever seen in my life!"

He pulled up short and shook his head. "For god's sake, Estella."

"Patriotic cats?" I pressed my hand to my chest. "The stripes and stylized flags weren't scary enough? They had to go and put those weird folk-art cats on it too?"

"You idiot. You scared me."

"Well, I think I may need therapy," I said. "That's the ugliest bathroom I've ever seen in my life."

He laughed. "Wait until you see the upstairs. Floral wallpaper, and the toilet and sinks are powder blue."

"Call Amanda now," I said, straight faced. "I'm not taking another step until she performs an exorcism on the bathrooms."

He burst out laughing. "Come on," he said, slinging an arm around my waist. "We'll face the horror together."

A half hour later, we sat together eating chicken and coleslaw off paper plates at a rickety café table and chairs that had been left on the house's mossy brick patio. Chauncey pulled a bottle of beer from a small cooler, twisted the top and passed it to me.

"Thanks," I said, taking a sip.

He got a bottle for himself and tapped it to mine. "Cheers."

I sat, comfortable and relaxed. "You know, the large side yards on either side of the house are good, because this house doesn't have much of a front yard."

"The back of the property goes into the woods," Chauncey said, pointing at it. "There's a shed back there that could use some work. But I'm excited about it."

"I'm figuring you put an offer in on it, otherwise we wouldn't be sitting here having a picnic on the side patio."

"I did, and it was accepted yesterday."

I'd had a forkful of coleslaw on the way to my mouth. But now I lowered the fork, as my stomach dropped to my shoes. "So, you'll be moving."

"Not for a while." He shrugged. "It'll take a few months to redo the kitchen and bathrooms. Still, once the renovations are finished, I'll be right here in the village. It's only a short drive away from the mansion."

"Short work commute," I managed to say.

"And I'll have great neighbors." He hooked a thumb toward Amanda's house.

"She's the best," I agreed.

While he talked enthusiastically about hoping to uncover a stone wall in the kitchen, I fought against a sudden sadness knowing he would soon be moving. I'd been getting used to seeing him all the time at the mansion. With a sigh, I picked back up my beer and took another sip. He was obviously in no hurry to leave. There'd been no attempt at seduction either and I was confused by the turn of events.

"You okay?" he asked as the uneven table shifted.

"Sure." I made a one-handed grab for the table and his beer stayed upright. Taking a breath, I figured I'd be blunt, and see how he reacted. "So, is this 'come check out this property with me' thing how you typically romance the ladies?"

He smiled and picked up his beer. "You mean looking at outdated kitchens and bathrooms didn't turn you on?"

"Absolutely." I batted my eyes. "You sure know how to seduce a woman, Marquette."

He'd been in mid-sip. Now he choked, coughed, and thumped a hand to his chest.

"Jesus, Estella!" He burst out laughing.

"Well?" I asked.

"God, you make me laugh." He wiped tears from his eyes. "I simply thought you'd be more comfortable tonight with a casual picnic somewhere private."

Where no one will see you together, a voice said in my mind.

Out loud I said, "Well I'm definitely a KFC and beer type of girl, as opposed to some fancy chick who only drinks champagne."

"Been there done that," he said, tossing me a wink.

"Too many violins and opera, and not enough football and rock and roll?" I guessed.

"Exactly," he said. "I could be happy never having to deal with all that society drivel ever again."

See? The voice slithered into my mind. *He doesn't think you're good enough for anything other than a dalliance. Deep down haven't you always known that?*

I frowned. Dalliance? Where in the hell had that word come from?

He can't help himself. He's a man. They will tell you whatever they think you want to hear, with the hopes of getting what they want...

"Stop it," I said.

"No, I'm serious, Estella," he said, unaware I'd been arguing with myself—sort of. "I've had my fill of society types and all their hypocrisy."

"Those shallow jet-setting bitches," I said, deadpan.

He grinned at that and rose halfway out of his chair. Leaning across the table he kissed me on the mouth. "I'm so glad you're here."

Instantly, that negative voice was gone, and I smiled. "I'm glad to be here too, Chauncey."

"So do you like the house?" he asked.

I smiled. "For what it's worth, I love the house."

"Good," he said and sat back down. "I can't wait to get started on the reno."

I never expected to be relaxed on my date with Chauncey Marquette. After we finished our food, I suggested that we drive into Alton and go to a home improvement store. Which obviously had been the right thing to do as he was thrilled with my suggestion.

We spent a couple hours looking at appliances, paint, and light fixtures. It was fun to see his enthusiasm for the house. Hand in hand, we strolled around the massive hardware store, eyeballing appliances and collecting paint swatches. Maybe it was old-fashioned, holding hands and shopping, but I found that I didn't mind. Not at all.

We arrived back at the mansion, and he walked me into the lobby of the eastern wing. "Thank you," he said.

I stopped short of the first stair. "What for?"

"For suggesting that we go to that home improvement store."

I shrugged. "You just bought a house. You're gonna need stuff. That's common sense."

He shifted closer and I tipped my face up to his, expecting and looking forward to his kiss, but he hesitated.

"Estella?" his voice was low.

"Yeah?"

"There's something I've been wanting to do all night, but I figured I should ask your permission first." His dark eyes were solemn, his facial expression was set. I couldn't tell if he was worried or simply determined.

"So, ask."

He stepped a bit closer. "I wanted to know if it was all right if I touch your hair when I kiss you."

My stomach flipped at his words.

"But," he continued, "you told me that you don't like hands near your face, and I worried that it would be triggering for you."

I simply stared at him.

"Estella?"

"I've never had someone ask if they could get their hands in my hair before."

Now he smiled. "Then I am delighted to discover that I'll be your first."

"I'm not a virgin, Chauncey," I said. "If that's what you're worried—"

The rest of my word were cut off because he swooped in and kissed me.

He tugged me in close, and I wrapped my arms around his back and opened my mouth to his kiss. Our tongues touched, and I felt his hands move up my back and slowly dip into my hair. He groaned, and it caused an answering tightening in my belly. The kiss deepened and now one of his hands cupped the back of my head, somehow creating the illusion that we were horizontal.

I'm not sure how long we stood there at the bottom of the steps kissing, but he was the one who pulled back first. With the smallest of nips to my bottom lip, Chauncey ended the kiss. His hands however stayed buried in my hair.

"Chauncey, I—"

"Goodnight, Estella." He kissed my forehead, slowly let his hands drop, and eased away.

Confused, I blinked at him. "You're going?"

He smiled slowly. "I'll see you tomorrow."

Shocked at his easy departure, I stared after him as he let himself back out the door. Once the door shut, I dropped down to the bottom step.

I'd half expected some sort of schmooze. I figured his proposition would be elegant, considering the sorts of circles he used to run in...but instead he'd simply been charming and easy company. The man had more style than I was used to.

He certainly had more class.

I started to chuckle at myself when I realized a small perverse part of me had been disappointed that he hadn't suggested we go back to his place. Instead, he'd left me wondering and wanting more.

I blew out a long breath. Truth was, that kiss had been a seduction all on its own.

CHAPTER SEVEN

The next week passed quietly. Gabriella continued to improve, and while she wasn't over the nausea, she was now able to keep broth and bland food down. What she needed was rest, so I took advantage of the cooler weather and ran my niece around outside as much as possible. Philippe got a plastic baby swing and hung it from a low branch of an old tree in the garden. Danielle loved it, and it proved to be a good distraction for her.

Chauncey started showing up in the family wing at Danielle's lunchtime. He claimed he was simply taking his lunch with us in order to get a break from the hotel office. However, he often kept Danielle entertained for a few minutes so I could take Gabriella some food and clean up the kitchen after our lunch was over.

In the afternoon Danielle napped, and I would toss in some laundry or prep dinner. Philippe typically worked straight through his lunch in order to finish his day earlier, to spend more time in the afternoon with Gabriella and Danielle.

After living at the mansion for these past weeks, I'd started to comprehend the sheer amount of *work* it took to maintain a house of this size. It was mind boggling, not to mention all the plotting, planning and effort the events venue, and hotel required. Nicole was a fiend in her PR office devising all sorts of strategies with Philippe to get more clients and bookings to the event venue.

I heard that Chauncey had come up with some other promotional event for the holidays, and now the winery and the hotel were working on that together. It made my head spin to overhear them talking about contract fees and deposits and the amount of money involved.

However, I quickly learned that while the money they'd make off the upcoming receptions and parties for the remainder of the year was impressive, the truth was that the Marquette's needed every dollar to help pay for all the renovations to the mansion over the past few years and to counter-balance their massive investment into *Trois Amis Winery.* Hopefully the winery, the hotel, and the event spaces would also begin to turn a profit very soon. I knew they were close, and that only had everyone working harder.

Amanda's wedding was now less than three weeks out. She and Zak had dropped by the mansion for a meeting on a cloudy afternoon with Nicole to go over the details of their ceremony—which was going to be outdoors on the western terrace—and of course their wedding reception, that would be held in the ballroom.

I stood and listened to Amanda as she went down her checklist with Nicole while Danielle toddled around the open space. My niece had been wild today, and I hoped if she ran around for a while, she would go down for a nap more easily later.

"I forgot about a backup plan in case it rains," Amanda said, rubbing her forehead, even as thunder rumbled outside. "What do you think, Estella? Should we use the smaller event room with the fireplace as an alternative ceremony location in case of inclement weather?"

Danielle ran screaming past us, and Zak made a grab for her. She bust a gut laughing when he chased her across the ballroom.

"I'm going to get you!" Zak growled, making the toddler laugh even harder.

I shifted back to Amanda and Nicole. "Sure, why not? I bet we could re-arrange the outdoor flowers all around the stone fireplace and stuff. It'd be cool."

Zak hoisted Danielle in the air. "I like the idea of a ceremony by the fireplace if it rains," he said over Danielle's giggles.

Amanda nodded. "All right let's have that be our back up plan."

My cell phone buzzed, and I pulled it out of my pocket. It was another phone call from Camilla. I let it go to voice mail. She'd been texting me that she wanted to talk at least once a day for the past week, and I had ignored all of her messages. Now she'd begun calling several times a day, and I let those go to voice mail. I was damn tempted to block her calls; she was becoming a pest.

Nicole left and Amanda closed her folder and tucked it into her bag. She watched Zak playing with Danielle from across the room and I gave her an elbow nudge.

"Hmm?" she said and finally focused on me.

"You got baby fever, girlfriend?"

"No, not really." Amanda smiled. "He's wonderful with children, isn't he?"

I smiled. "Yeah. You got yourself a good one."

"We need to get going," she said. "I have a meeting with the florist today. She's going to coordinate with Max and his gardening center for the pumpkins and potted chrysanthemums to decorate the reception space with."

Zak carried Danielle over and I took her from him. "Happy flower and pumpkin shopping," I said to the couple. "We'll see you later."

With a wave, Zak and Amanda exited out the doors to the western terrace and I popped Danielle on my hip, began to hum, and danced her around and then out of the ballroom. With a spin, we began waltzing down the hall.

"Hey, Estella!" a cheerful voice called.

Caught, I smiled. "Hey." I stopped my attempt at formal dancing and instead stood and chatted up Jaxon, one of the servers and assistant bartender.

But that didn't last too long. Danielle had started to

squirm, so I excused us and headed for the family wing. I waved to the front desk clerk as we passed, moved farther along the hall past the museum room, and finally I hit the code to the door that separated the hotel reception space from the family wing.

"Daddy?" Danielle said hopefully.

"Daddy's at work," I said, earning an instant pout from my niece.

Philippe's office, as well as Nicole's, was off the eastern lobby, but I knew that he and Chauncey were having a meeting with the event staff today. So instead of peeking in, I headed directly up the stairs.

That did not sit well with Danielle. A full-blown meltdown was moments away. I jogged up the steps, paused to put in the code at the security gate, and went through as fast as possible, hoping to clear the public area before she totally let loose.

Once I gained the third floor, I entered the nursery and changed her diaper. We settled in a comfy chair with her favorite book and the toddler's mood changed. With relief, I began to read a story to her. We made it through four pages before her eyes began to grow heavy.

"There you are." Gran appeared in the nursery doorway. "I was visiting Gabriella and wanted to see you—"

I held up a finger in a bid to have my grandmother wait. She nodded and fell silent. Rising to my feet with the baby in my arms, I laid her down in her bed and she rolled over. Covering her with a light blanket, I picked up the nursery monitor and left the room.

Gran stood waiting in the hall. "Why don't we go out on the terrace, before the storm rolls in?"

I nodded and secured the baby gate before moving out to the balcony with my grandmother.

"They certainly have a lot of baby gates around here," she said, walking over to take a seat on one of the lounge chairs.

"Well, yeah." I went to join her. "There's the security gate to keep folks out of the family wing, and while it's a pain to have to put it up all the time, better to have a baby gate over the nursery door than to have Danielle toddle out and fall down the stairs…or try and climb the ones to the new primary bedroom."

"I have some news," Gran said, making herself comfortable in the outdoor chair.

"What's up?" I asked, placing the baby monitor speaker on the outdoor table.

She smiled. "Camilla and Jacob are expecting a baby early next summer."

I took a seat beside my grandmother. "That's nice."

My grandmother gave me a steady look. "It is, isn't it? They are very excited."

"I'll bet," I said, trying to drum up any enthusiasm.

"Camilla's been feeling a bit tired and peaked, but she's not dealing with morning sickness as severe as Gabriella's, fortunately."

There was more. I felt it in my gut. The baby

announcement wasn't the real reason my grandmother had dropped by.

"There's more news." She took a deep breath. "The rental property Camilla and Jacob had hoped to purchase didn't work out, and so they will be taking ownership of the Midnight family farmhouse. They will be moving in before the end of October."

It took a second for the importance of that statement to sink in. It was important because there were only three bedrooms on the second floor of the farmhouse. The largest room was for the couple, one was for Jaimie, and of course the last would be needed for their new baby.

Which meant there was no longer any room for me.

I swallowed past a lump in my throat. "I see."

"Now I realize this all seems a bit awkward..." my grandmother began.

"I suppose it's a good thing that I already moved out," I said. "It'll make their move-in less problematic."

"Estella." Gran's voice was censuring. "You know better than that."

I shifted in my chair and sent her a hard look. "Do I?"

"The house must stay in the family," Gran said. "The property is held in a trust and can only be passed to a —"

"*Legitimate* member of the family?"

She scowled. "Stop finishing my sentences."

I shrugged. "I've been told it's an annoying habit of

mine."

"I'm trying to explain—"

"That I'm being booted out?" I finished for her. "I get it."

Gran tossed her hands in the air. "You are completely misunderstanding the situation."

Deeply hurt, I stood and went to the railing. "Oh, I understand the *situation* with Camilla perfectly," I argued. "First, Gabriella is her sister—not mine—and now she needs me out of the way and has sent you here to do her dirty work for her."

"No, that's not it." Gran stood and joined me at the railing. "Sweetheart, Camilla and I had always talked about her becoming the caretaker of the property someday."

I turned my head away from her and considered the view while she continued to speak.

"It's simple really," she said. "Dru and Garrett have their home, Gabriella and Philippe have here. But now, Camilla and Jacob need a space for their growing family. It all works out beautifully. Camilla becomes the next daughter of Midnight to hold the land, and I won't be burdened with the sole upkeep of the gardens and the house. I don't mind admitting that it's become too much for me to keep up with."

They want you gone, a familiar voice said in my mind. *Your sisters have their own families now, and you are nothing but a burden to them all. You're different. Nothing like the rest of them. A single unmarried woman. An embarrassment...*

I shook my head and tuned back into what my grandmother was saying.

"Camilla wanted to tell you her big news herself," she was saying. "The day she and Drusilla came up to visit Gabriella; she told her sisters about the baby and their plans for the farmhouse. She wanted to share this news with you too, but she said that you've been avoiding her."

See? The sisters all plotted against you...

That voice hit me hard, and a single tear escaped. Embarrassed, I quickly brushed it away. What was with me? I never cried.

"Estella," my grandmother was saying, "we simply thought that since you were already staying with Gabriella and her family—"

"Will Camilla at least allow you to stay in your old room downstairs after she takes over?" I asked bitterly.

My grandmother recoiled. "Of course, she will."

"*You* may stay. How generous of her." I smiled thinly. "Well, this *is* awkward, isn't it?"

"I don't understand," she said. "What on earth are you talking about?"

I glared. "Don't play the confused old lady card with me, Priscilla. It's insulting."

"Priscilla?" She jerked back. "What happened to you calling me Gran?"

Forced into the role of cook and nursemaid...Don't let what happened to me happen to you, a voice whispered in my ear. *They'll use you, Estella. Take away everything that you love...*

I tried to push those intruding thoughts away. Shaking my head, I discovered that my grandmother was speaking to me.

"Estella?" she said hesitantly.

They are using you...

My stomach flipped over as the truth hit home, and damn, it wasn't very pretty. "Let's be honest with each other," I said. "If I were to suddenly walk out and stop helping Gabriella's family, you'd all be in a hell of a pickle. Philippe would have to probably hire someone full time to cook and take care of the baby, and that'd sure be a bummer. Especially since I've been doing all of this for *free*."

Philippe stepped on the balcony. "I didn't mean to eavesdrop," he said, "but I was becoming concerned. What is wrong?"

"Oh, well that's absolutely perfect!" I said, firing up. "And here's your backup! Damn it, Priscilla, were you *that* worried that I'd cause a scene?"

"*Excusez-moi?*" Philippe raised his eyebrows. "What is happening here?"

"Nothing much." I crossed my arms over my chest. "I'm simply being put firmly in my place by the *señora*."

"Estella!" my grandmother snapped. "I do not appreciate your tone. You are deliberately misunderstanding everything!"

Philippe stepped between us. "I think everyone should calm down."

"No worries, Philippe." I shrugged. "I've been homeless before. I can figure something out."

"Homeless? What in the hell just happened?" Philippe demanded.

"All things considered," I said evenly, "I suppose it was very generous of you to have allowed me to stay in your home for as long as you did."

On the baby monitor I heard Danielle wake and cry.

"Lala?" she called.

Automatically, Philippe turned toward the monitor.

I grabbed up the baby monitor and handed it to him. "I apologize, Philippe, for outstaying my welcome."

"Estella, please," Philippe began as rain began to fall. "Gabriella and I spoke about this and we—"

I spoke right over him. "Danielle will be wanting supper." My voice cracked, and I cleared my throat against it. "There's beef stew waiting for you in the crockpot."

"Estella," Philippe said, as a red flush rode up his cheeks. "Wait. You don't understand."

Seeing his embarrassment clinched it for me. *Jesus,* I realized, *Philippe had been coming to tell me that he wanted me to leave too.*

I was seconds away from crying, and mortified, I walked out the door and into the hallway.

"Lala!" Danielle cried.

Hearing the baby broke my heart. Blindly, I ran

down the stairs. The security gate on the first-floor landing swung open as if by magick, and without breaking stride I rushed down the last set of stairs, made the lobby, and sprinted toward the door to shove it open.

Go! The voice in my head screamed at me.

Run!

Get away!

Mindlessly, I did as I was told. I tore down the hill, past the winery show room, and hit the pavement of the cliff road that went toward the village. That sprinkle quickly became rain, and with a crack of thunder, the rain morphed into a torrential downpour.

Still, I ran. The last time I'd run so far or fast I'd been a teenager running from the cops. Pausing only for a moment, I swiped the hair from my eyes to better see the road. Strong winds whipped the trees around and drove the rain sideways. It was getting worse. Panting for breath, I eyeballed the line of trees looking for cover. I couldn't stay out in this storm.

A car honked and pulled over to the curb directly in front of me.

"Estella?" Jaxon, the bartender, stuck his head out the window and peered at me through the shower. "Hey girl, what are you doing out in a thunderstorm?"

"Would you believe that I needed to clear my head?" I said, jogging to his car.

"Get in!" Jaxon said, as lightning flashed and thunder boomed simultaneously.

I heard a loud crack and spun in time to see a large tree come down. It fell across the road, maybe twenty yards behind us, and landed with a loud thud. That was it. I opened the rear passenger door and jumped in. "Shit!" I said, wiping my dripping hair from my face.

Jaxon turned to look at me over his shoulder. "You didn't get fired too, did you?"

"Fired?" My jaw dropped. "Christ Jesus, they *were* a busy bunch up at the mansion today, weren't they?"

"I know, right?" he said. "Do you need a ride somewhere?"

"I sure the hell do." I nodded. "Can you drop me off in the village?"

"You bet," he said.

A few minutes later, I stood on Amanda's back deck. It continued to dump rain and her car was not in the driveway; she was probably still out with Zak. I reached for my phone in my back pocket to call her and discovered that it was also soaked and completely dead. "Perfect," I muttered.

I didn't think she would mind if I went in. I started to reach for the doorknob, and a crack of thunder echoed overhead, almost like a warning. The house was enchanted. Amanda said she felt it was a sort of spirit, but whatever it was, *it* was intelligent and very protective, so long as you were a welcomed guest.

I yanked my hand back. "Okay, okay," I said. "Spirit of the house, may I please come in? I've literally got nowhere else to go."

The door unlocked by itself and swung open.

I stepped over the threshold and hesitated. When the house didn't object, I moved farther into the kitchen and the door shut behind me.

The lights in the kitchen became brighter, and the coffee maker on the counter gurgled to life. It was the house's way of welcoming me. Tears sprang to my eyes, and I let them fall. "*Gracias,*" I said.

"Meow?" Nyx pranced into the kitchen and skidded to a halt. The scruffy black cat looked me up and down.

"I don't want anyone other than Amanda to know that I'm here," I said to the cat and to the ever-present spirit of the house.

In answer, the lights pulsed brighter, and the land line phone on the counter began to ring. My sneakers squished as I moved across the floor. I stared at the phone for a moment, and when it kept ringing, I reached for it. Picking up the receiver, I held it to my ear but did not speak.

"Estella?" Amanda's voice came through clearly.

"I'm here," I said.

"What happened?" she asked.

Instead of answering her, I asked, "Hey, is it okay if I take a shower and borrow some dry clothes?"

"Of course." Her voice was soothing. "Be at home. Help yourself to whatever you need."

"Thank you, Amanda," I said. "And if anyone asks, you haven't heard from me."

"All right." Her voice was calm. "Are you certain

that you are okay?"

"Physically I'm fine," I said. "Emotionally, not so much."

"I can be home in an hour," she said. "There are sweatpants and casual tops in the bottom drawer of my dresser."

"I appreciate it," I said, toeing off my sneakers.

"See you soon," she said and hung up.

"I'm going to hit the shower," I said to Nyx. "Borrow some of Amanda's clothes."

With a chirping sound, the cat scrambled up the steps to the second floor. I placed my shoes by the back door and followed Nyx to the guest bathroom. The cat hopped up on the sink, and I patted her head. I shivered once and stripped out of my dripping clothes. Turning the water to hot, I stepped in the shower.

After scrubbing up, I wrapped my hair and then myself in towels. Going to Amanda's room, I took a pair of sweats and an old schleppy shirt out of her dresser. My toes were freezing, so I hazarded a guess and found her sock drawer. I added a pair of fuzzy socks, too.

Scrubbing a hand through my drying hair, I padded back downstairs with my wet clothes and towels and went straight to her laundry room off the kitchen. I got the laundry going, shuffled back to the kitchen, and discovered a plate of cookies sitting out on the counter. For a second, I paused. The cookies hadn't been there before.

"Those for me?" I asked the house.

The lights above me brightened slightly in answer.

I grabbed one and took a big bite. "Oatmeal raisin," I mumbled around a mouthful. "My favorite."

I did as Amanda suggested and made myself at home. Selecting my favorite tea from the canister on the counter, I snagged a big mug, dropped in the tea bag, and put the cup in the machine. I hit the button for hot water and tried to finger comb out any tangles from my hair while the mug filled up.

In short order, I was sitting on Amanda's couch sipping my tea and polishing off the last of the cookies. Nyx sprawled belly up on the sofa next to me, and I rested back against the cushions and finally let my shoulders drop.

Now, safely away from the mansion, I went back over the events of the afternoon. Camilla was pregnant and apparently diva-like behavior went along with it. Had Drusilla known in advance about her sister's plans for the farmhouse? I doubted it. She was far too busy with her new family to have time to plot and plan with Camilla.

Now when it came to sister number two: I knew for a fact Gabriella was totally unaware. She'd been pretty busy either being sick from being pregnant with twins or trying to keep her food down, while she did whatever she could to make sure she stayed pregnant. As to Philippe, his whole face had flushed red at my confrontation with Gran—Priscilla, I corrected myself.

He'd been mortified, and currently I had no idea if that was because he'd hoped to find a less dramatic way to ask me to go after Gabriella recovered, or if it was because he was ashamed to have Camilla's nefarious intentions revealed...

"Nefarious?" I asked myself out loud. "Where did that word come from?" I glanced around Amanda's home. The moody academic vibe of the home was probably getting to me. Either that, or I was absorbing a bigger vocabulary from hanging around a librarian.

CHAPTER EIGHT

I polished off my tea and kicked back. Outside, the thunder cracked, and the rain kept right on dumping. I was comfortable sitting in the gloom, but the candles Amanda kept everywhere suddenly flickered to life. I heard a *whoosh* and saw that the fire in the grate had sprung to life as well.

I smiled. The storm might be wailing outside, but inside Amanda's house I was warm, safe, and dry. Nyx roused herself and climbed up on me. She stretched out, resting her head against my shoulder, and began to purr.

I passed my hand over her head and the cat burrowed in. Exhausted, I held the cat and shut my eyes for a moment. "I'm gonna rest my eyes for a second," I said to Nyx and dozed right off.

I jerked awake as soon as Amanda let herself in the back door.

"Estella?" she called out.

"I'm in the living room," I answered. Straightening up, I wiped the drool off my face. I'd gone down hard.

Amanda stopped in the archway. "Well, you look like shit."

I raised my eyebrows. "You know, I think I can count the number of times on one hand that I've ever heard you swear in front of me."

"I hang around you too much, *chica*. You're rubbing off on me. Yesterday I pinched my fingers in a drawer and swore in Spanish."

"Oh yeah? What'd you say."

Amanda rattled off a very salty phrase in perfectly accented Spanish.

"Wow." My lips twitched. "Do you even know what that means?"

She walked over and sat beside me. "Of course, I do. I looked it up."

I laughed, and for some reason, it turned into a sob. Hearing it, I pressed a hand over my mouth.

"Estella," she said gently. "Who hurt you?"

"Camilla and Priscilla. They booted me out of the farmhouse." I pressed my lips together hard, doing my best not to cry. "I don't know what I did wrong. Maybe they got tired of having me around... I think Philippe was getting ready to ask me to leave too."

"I've got you, cousin." Amanda held open her arms. "You're not alone."

That simple statement broke me. Dropping my head on her shoulder, I let the tears come.

***

The storm passed. Not only the thunderstorm that had rolled through western Illinois, but also my emotional storm as well. I spent the night at Amanda's house, and except for her, I spoke to no one. The following morning the sun came out, and I discovered my clothes were now clean, dry, and folded at the end of the bed I'd slept in.

I got up immediately, got redressed, and made the bed up in the guestroom where I'd stayed. Wandering down to the kitchen, I thought I could make breakfast as a way to say thank you. I heard Amanda moving around upstairs, and so I grabbed a K-cup, slapped it in the machine and got her coffee going.

She appeared in the doorway in plaid pajama bottoms and an old worn t-shirt. Her hair was everywhere, and her eyes were blurry behind her glasses. "Morning," she said.

"How do you feel about scrambled eggs with cheese?" I asked, whisking four eggs in a bowl with a fork.

"I feel fabulous about anything I don't have to cook."

I set the bowl down and passed her the mug of coffee. "Cool. Have a seat. This won't take me but a couple of minutes."

In short order, I had the bread toasted, a mug of tea for myself, and two plates full of toast and eggs sprinkled with cheddar cheese. I plunked them down and joined my cousin at the table.

Amanda sampled the eggs. "This is wonderful. But you don't have to cook while you're staying here. You know that, right?"

"I know, but I wanted to. As a way to say thanks for letting me crash in the guest room."

Amanda took a sip of coffee. "You can stay here as long as you need."

"Thank you," I said, "but with you and Zak getting married in a couple of weeks, I don't want to be intruding on the honeymoon."

"Regardless," she said. "You will always have a home with me."

"And I appreciate that." I sighed. "It dawned on me last night, that I suppose I'd better start looking for a job. It'll have to be in the village since I don't own a car."

"I wouldn't worry about that right now," Amanda said.

I nodded and we ate in companionable silence. Honestly, the push I'd felt to get the hell out of the mansion still felt justified. They'd all turned against me after all. Once I finished my eggs, I sat back. "What time do you go into the library today?"

"Not until noon," she said. "In the meantime, I should tell you that Gabriella, Philippe, and Drusilla have all called my cell, looking for you."

"I hope you didn't tell them that I was here."

Amanda peered at me from over the top of her

glasses. "I said that they called. I didn't say that I had spoken to them."

Mollified at her answer, I nodded, rose to my feet, and gathered the empty dishes.

"As far as I'm concerned, they can continue to wonder and worry for another couple of hours." Amanda crossed her arms over her chest. "The guilt will do them all a world of good."

"I can't argue with that," I said, taking everything to the sink.

"I went over this a dozen times in my mind last night," Amanda said. "I would have never imagined Camilla would be so insensitive. Sending Priscilla to tell you that you can't move back to the farmhouse?"

"Yeah," I said. "After a year of them all insisting, *this is your home too,* only to be told: Sorry, change of plans. There's no more room." I shook my head. "It was a hell of a nasty surprise, and I never even saw it coming."

"Neither did I," Amanda admitted.

I filled up the sink with hot water and squirted in some dish soap. "Don't know what made me angrier, the fact that I was caught completely off guard, or that they were able to hurt me so badly. The worst part was Priscilla acting as if I'd hurt *her* feelings by my reaction."

Amanda rolled her eyes. "How in the world did they think you were going to react?"

The land line on the counter began to ring. That

phone line was only used to contact Amanda for magickal emergencies.

"The *Bat Phone* is ringing," I said. "I wonder what new magickal baddie is threatening Ames Crossing today?"

"Perhaps it's the ghost of the Reaver," Amanda said, rising to her feet and going to answer it.

"Who or what the hell is a Reaver?" I asked.

"An infamous river pirate, who killed indiscriminately in this area a few hundred years ago." She picked up the receiver. "Tell you about it later."

"Okay," I said.

"Hello?" Amanda spoke into the phone. "Good morning, Zakary." She paused for a few moments to listen. "Yes, she's safe, and staying with me for the time being."

I had been washing the dishes; but now hearing the conversation, I slapped the water off to better listen.

"Oh, is he?" Amanda's smile was razor thin. "Well, you can tell Philippe that filing a missing person's report is not required."

"Jesus," I muttered. "First, I'm family, then I'm not. They basically tossed me out and then *afterward* they decided I was missing?"

Amanda raised a hand in a silent plea for me to be quiet. With a nod, I shut up.

"Yes," she said into the phone, "I do realize that they'll figure out soon enough where Estella is. However, I would appreciate if you did not share her current location. I think it best if we let things cool off. She's not in any shape for a confrontation with her family at this time."

While Amanda continued to talk with Zak, I took the dish rag, dunked it in the water and wiped up the counters. After a couple more minutes, Amanda said goodbye and hung up the phone.

"You might be interested to know," she began, "that your brother-in-law is currently down at the sheriff's station trying to list you as a missing person."

"Seriously?"

"Mm hmm." Amanda nodded.

I went back to the sink and slapped the water back on. "Never expected that." I scrubbed a plate, rinsed it, and set it in the drainer. "Guess someone feels guilty."

Amanda retrieved a towel from a drawer and stood beside me.

"It says a lot that Philippe is the one who is there," she said. "According to Zakary he was shouting and swearing in French at the desk sergeant, when he was informed that a person had to be missing for at least twenty-four hours."

I did a double take at the news. "Philippe yelled at the desk sergeant?"

"Correct." Amanda picked up a dish and rubbed the towel over it. "While the other deputies were trying to reason with him, Zakary called me. Now that we've spoken, he'll go and talk privately to Philippe and let him know that you're safe."

"Okay."

"Now Chauncey, on the other hand..."

Her words had me dropping the plate back into the water.

"He called me last night," she said. "Seems he knew exactly where you were. All he wanted was to make sure that you were okay."

"He did?"

Amanda gave me a hip bump. "Yes, he did."

"Oh, well, I suppose he was feeling...awkward." I scrubbed hard at the dish. "You know, about the uh, situation."

"He was pretty angry, actually."

I rinsed the dish and passed it to Amanda. "He was?"

Amanda nodded. "He was. Apparently, he and Philippe had words."

I'd been reaching for the cutlery in the bottom of the sink, but now I froze. "He argued with his brother over me?"

Amanda smiled. "I hear that Gabriella called Camilla and chewed her out, too."

"Gabriella is supposed to be resting!" I said. "She needs to take it easy. Her blood pressure is elevated and —"

"I find it interesting," Amanda said calmly, "that your first thought is for Gabriella's health."

"For fuck's sake!" I snapped. "She's fighting hard to stay pregnant with the twins. Of course, I'm worried about her."

Amanda smiled at me. "You make an excellent point."

I scowled at her. "Are you doing that reverse psychology shit on me?"

"Never," she said. "I would, however, like to give you a heads up that Chauncey will be dropping by the house today after I leave for work. He told me he wanted to speak to you in private, so I told him he was welcome."

"Oh," I said nervously. "Well, shit."

"He's not angry with you, Estella. He's worried because he knows you're hurt."

"Huh." Deep down I was sort of pleased to find out that Chauncey was worried about me, but still... "I don't know what to do with that," I admitted.

"Well, you have a few hours to figure it out," Amanda said.

All I could do was nod.

***

I could admit that the thought of seeing Chauncey alone, after everything that had happened yesterday, was making me nervous as hell. I'd been pacing in the living room for the past fifteen minutes, wondering what to say or what this even meant for us going forward.

"It's stupid to build a future after one date with the guy, Estella," I muttered.

Catching my reflection in the mirror above Amanda's mantle, I scowled at myself. There I stood in jeans and an old, faded shirt that had seen better days. I'd done my best with my face, knowing he was coming over. I'd even borrowed mascara and powder from Amanda, but our skin tones were so different that anything else was pointless.

I look rough, I decided, *and down on my luck.*

I couldn't imagine what he'd want to say to me. Or, honestly, what he even saw in me. Turning away from my reflection, all I knew for certain was that I was anxious to see him. That I *needed* to see him.

I heard the kitchen door open and him walk inside. He paused in the archway to the living room and our eyes met.

"Hey," I said.

His hair was tousled, and his eyes were dark and concerned as they swept over me. This gorgeous man, who'd seen the world, who'd once played with the rich and famous, had come to see me. To check on me.

I'd always prided myself on being able to stand on my own. But now, all I could think was how badly I wanted to throw myself into his arms and simply be held; to be comforted, and to hear him say that everything would be all right.

I wanted him to love me as much as I loved him.

I was in love with Chauncey Marquette. The words flashed into my mind, and my heart gave one hard leap in response. Truthfully, I'd always known it had been my fate, but I'd been simply too afraid to admit it to myself.

As I stared at him, Chauncey pulled his leather jacket off, tossed it to the side and marched straight to me. "Estella," he said and reached out to pull me close.

Exactly as I'd hoped he would.

"I'm glad you're here," I said, wrapping my arms around his waist.

He pressed a kiss to my hair. "I'm so sorry."

My heart melted. "It's not your fault that Camilla wants me gone."

He pulled back to meet my eyes. "You're not going anywhere."

"Truthfully, I can't go anywhere." I half-laughed. "I don't have a car—"

"Estella," he began.

"Or even money for a plane ticket." I kept right on talking. "I'm definitely going to have to find a job though, because—"

"Shut up, Estella," he said and silenced me with a kiss.

The kiss was everything. The feelings for him that I'd held back for the past year rushed to the surface, and I poured them into our kiss. This—whatever we had started—would probably never last. *But just once,* I thought desperately, *what would it be like to have someone accept me for who I truly am, and love me anyway?*

I told myself to be grateful for any time I would have

with him. *Maybe I could dazzle him with sex. Maybe he'd be so happy with me as a lover that he'd want me to stay in his life, long term...* My thoughts broke off when he groaned into my mouth.

"I want you," he said. "So much."

Sliding my arms around his neck, I pressed closer. "I want you too," I said, between kisses. "I don't want to wait anymore."

"Are you sure?" he asked.

I nipped his bottom lip. "Very sure."

His hands slid down and around to my butt and he boosted me up. I wrapped my legs around his waist, and he carried me across the living room floor.

Our kiss continued until he paused on the first riser. He set me down and, after taking his hand, I tugged him to follow me. We raced up the stairs, to the bedroom I'd been staying in. I might have been new to the emotions of love, but the physicality of it I completely understood. As soon as he cleared the door, I shut it and locked it behind us.

"Estella." His voice was low and there was a light in his eyes I'd never seen before. Responding to it, I pulled my shirt over my head and flung it on the floor.

"I need you," I said, unbuttoning and unzipping my jeans. "Right now, Chauncey."

"I've imagined us together so many times," he said softly.

"Is that right?" I asked, stepping out of the denim. "Probably not as often as *I've* thought about it." I walked to the bed and yanked back the quilt.

"You might be surprised," he said, unbuttoning his own shirt.

I sat on the edge of the bed and sent him a slow smile. "Well get on over here and show me, why don't you?

He stepped closer, and I tossed my hair behind my back. Unhooking the front clasp of my bra, I shrugged free of it and tossed it at him.

I knew what came next. He'd smile and swoop in. We'd wrestle across the bed, until we were both completely naked. And then finally, finally he'd be deep inside me, and this terrible ache would lessen.

He simply stood there, smiling at me as I sat and waited for him. "You're beautiful, Estella."

I felt myself blush at the compliment, not knowing what to say in response.

He eased forward and kissed me tenderly. Chauncey lifted his mouth from mine, straightened and let his shirt drop to the floor. I got an eyeful of his chest and abs, which were more defined than I'd imagined. Taking his time, he began to unbuckle and unzip, and I scooted back against the pillows to make room for him.

"Chauncey." I sent him a confident smile and patted the empty spot beside me. "Get in the bed."

He shoved his slacks and briefs down and began to climb across the bed toward me. When he hooked his thumbs in my panties, I smiled. He tugged them free, and I opened my arms expecting him to cover me immediately.

Slowly, he settled over me and I opened my legs to accommodate his hips. I was shocked when instead of sliding home, he rested his weight on his elbows. "Are you okay with my hands here?" he asked, slowly framing my face with both of his hands.

I blinked in surprise at the request. "Chauncey?"

"Is this okay?" he asked again, brushing my hair back from my face.

I nodded. "Yes."

With a soft sigh, he whispered my name. He pressed kisses across my forehead, sweetly and slowly, but he made no other move to claim me.

I could feel him against me. He was huge and ready to go. I shifted again. "What are you waiting for?" I asked, genuinely confused.

Instead of answering me, he began to kiss his way across my jaw and down my throat. "So beautiful," he murmured

Undone by the gentleness, I lay there and trembled. Chauncey kissed his way down my body, praising my curves and sampling each of my breasts. He lingered there and eventually his hands followed, and they were gentle as well. He cruised lower, and with the most tender of touches and kisses he had me right on the brink. Before I could go over the edge, he changed course and began to work his way back up toward my mouth.

Finally, he lowered his lips to mine. This time, he

kissed me deeply. His tongue swept in and claimed every corner of my mouth, and then finally, he eased inside me.

His hands found mine and our fingers wove together. I groaned as he slowly pressed forward carefully, stretching me to the limit. Once he was completely sheathed, he stayed still for a moment allowing my inner muscles to adjust. Still his kiss went on, and I was literally shaking, waiting for him to move again. When at last he did, his strokes were slow and sultry, matching tempo with his kisses.

I pulled my mouth from his, gasping for air. Wrapping my arms and legs around him, I held on as he continued to move. Chauncey's pace was unhurried, and I'd never had a lover who'd filled me so completely or taken such care before. I bucked against him once, but his pace never changed, nor did it waver. He was relentless. But in the gentlest way I'd ever known.

My orgasm built slowly, and when it hit, my head fell back and tears welled up in my eyes. He reached completion a second after I did, and it was both devastating and beautiful all at the same time.

***

I woke up and found Chauncey staring at me and smiling.

"What?" I asked.

He was propped up on one elbow and our faces were

close together. "You sleep with your mouth open."

"I sleep like I'm dead dog tired."

He wiggled his eyebrows. "Did I wear you out?"

"It's been a crazy couple of days." I yawned and scooted closer. "I don't know what's going to happen next, but I'm glad to be here with you, Chauncey."

He pressed a kiss to my forehead. The simple act had my breath catching in my throat. It took me a moment, but I was able to casually turn my head and check the time. With a sigh of relief, I dropped my head to the pillow again.

"When does Amanda get home?" he asked.

"In about three hours," I said.

"Oh, *really*?" he asked cheerfully, and began to nuzzle at my breasts.

I slanted him a look. "You ready for a second round?"

"Estella, you have such a romantic way with words." His tone was as dry as toast.

"You want romance, Marquette?" I pushed on his shoulder, and he obligingly rolled to his back. Tossing a leg over, I straddled him. Then I leaned in and kissed the crap out of him.

After a couple of minutes, I lifted my mouth from his. "How's that for romance?" I asked.

"Works for me," he said.

"I thought it might."

"I want to put my hands in your hair." His voice was low and his eyes steady on mine as he spoke. "May I?"

"You may," I said.

While Chauncey ran his hands up my shoulders and into my hair, I slid down over him, taking him inside me. Whispering my name, he drew me down and we kissed again. He fisted his hands in my hair, and our kiss went on and on, as we moved together more urgently this time. Somehow it wasn't only physical, there was a compelling power here. This was an irresistibly emotional experience as well.

Chauncey Marquette had managed to show me a side of physical love that I'd never known. It shook me deeply and made me realize that—for me at least—there was no going back. I would always love him.

I could only pray that maybe he would grow to love me in return.

CHAPTER NINE

When Amanda had arrived home at the end of her shift, Chauncey and I were standing side-by-side in her kitchen, making supper.

He'd done the whole pasta and salad thing again and I'd told him it was such a typical guy meal. He'd laughed at that and relegated me to the position of fetch and carry girl. But to be honest, I was so damned happy with him *and* with us having finally gotten together, that I truly didn't mind.

I figured Amanda had taken one look at us and had known, but she had too much style to tease me or say anything about it in front of him. Chauncey stayed for a while, and after supper I walked him outside. We kissed goodbye on Amanda's back deck, and he promised to call me in the morning.

"Might be a problem. My phone is shot," I said. "From being in all that rain."

"That explains why you never answered my calls or texts."

"Yeah, sorry." I shrugged. "I'll see about getting a replacement."

"Let me see what I can do."

"Meaning what?" I asked.

"Get some rest," he said by way of an answer, and with a final kiss, he left.

The next morning after Amanda headed into the village to open the library, Chauncey dropped off a brand-new cell phone for me. My jaw dropped when he handed me the bag, and even though I tried to tell him that wasn't necessary, he refused to listen to any of my arguments. In fact, he tugged me to him and silenced me with a scorching hot kiss.

Eventually, he lifted his mouth from mine. "This is the part where you say, thank you, Chauncey."

I shook my head, trying to get my brains to re-engage. "Thank you, Chauncey. I'll pay you back for the phone."

He frowned. "It's a gift."

"I'm not the kind of girl who needs or expects gifts from her lover," I argued.

"I never thought you were," he said. "But you *need* a phone. I programmed my number in for you."

"That was smart. Saves me the trouble."

He studied me suspiciously, as if expecting another argument. Finally, he said, "I'll call you later. I need to go back up to the mansion. We have staff meetings today."

"Did you really fire all the bartenders and wait

staff?"

"No." He checked his watch. "Who told you that?"

"I hear things," I said.

"I let Ned, the bar manager, go. There's a huge problem with his attitude, and major discrepancies with the bar's inventory."

"You got yourself a free pour bar?" I asked.

Chauncey did a double take. "Meaning?"

"Theft is often the biggest problem at bars," I said. "It comes from not writing or ringing the drinks up, or the bartender giving away free drinks hoping to score bigger tips. Bottom line, you have no way to calculate how much alcohol is being poured."

Chauncey stared at me for a long minute.

"What?" I said. "I worked as a bartender for years. I know how to run a bar."

"Hmmm." He rubbed a hand over his chin. "I have something I want to run by you later. A proposition."

I grinned. "Yes, I'll have sex with you again."

"That's not what I meant." He laughed and pressed a quick kiss to my cheek. "Enjoy the phone."

"You don't have to buy me gifts, Chauncey. All I want is you." I went up on my toes to kiss him and I lingered over it. "What time is your meeting?"

"In twenty-five minutes," he said.

I nipped his bottom lip. "Wanna get in a quickie?"

He groaned. "Don't tease me."

I reached down and ran my fingers lightly over his crotch. "Baby, I never tease."

"I have to go," he said, yet his hands were now covering my breasts.

My eyes locked on his. "You really should stay."

Ten minutes later...

"I can't believe we had sex in the kitchen," Chauncey said as he began to straighten his clothes.

I stayed where I was sitting on the counter. "That was great." I sighed happily. "I think we might have just set a land speed record."

"That's not particularly flattering."

I smiled. "Are you kidding? That was *awesome*."

He shook his head at my words and checked his watch. "Damn it, I've got to leave right now, or I won't make my meeting."

"So go to your meeting." I swung my feet. "Be a businessman."

He tucked his winery polo into his casual slacks and zipped up. "I have no bloody idea how I'm going to be able to concentrate today."

"I bet you have notes on your laptop."

He dropped a quick kiss on my mouth. "See you tonight?"

I gave him a sassy smile. "You betcha."

He made it to the kitchen door and stopped to turn around and look at me. "Jesus," he breathed. "All I'm going to see in my mind for the rest of the day, is you sitting there naked on the counter."

Deliberately, I arched my back. "Then stay with me."

"I just had you," he said, staring at my breasts, "and now I want you all over again."

His words thrilled me, but I fought not to let it show too much. Not if I wanted to win his heart. "Talk is cheap." I playfully tilted my head to one side. "Come on over here and show me how much you want me."

"I'm going," he said, but didn't move.

There was a look in his eye, much less civilized than he'd shown me before. Delighted by it, I held my breath and waited, but then the kitchen door eased open all on its own.

I suppose Amanda's enchanted house had decided that he should go to his meeting after all.

"I'll call you later," he said.

"Okay."

He gave me one last simmering look and let himself out.

After I heard his car start up, I hopped down from the counter with a grin. Gathering up my clothes, I made a mental note to scrub down the counter and headed for the shower.

***

The cell phone was a lot fancier than my old one and I spent a couple hours setting everything up. I had to look up a few things on Amanda's laptop to figure it out, but eventually I got it. I sent Chauncey a text letting him know that I had the phone up and running and told him I hoped he wasn't too distracted during his meetings.

Then I sent him a photo of the kitchen counter.

He texted back: *Very funny.*

Chuckling to myself, I set the phone down on the table and began a search online for a new job. Amanda had said they could use a part time clerk in the library, but I couldn't see myself in the library. It would do in a pinch, but I hoped for something else.

Sipping at a mug of tea, I scrolled my way through the local job listings while Nyx kept me company. She sat on the table rubbing her face on the laptop's screen.

When the kitchen door suddenly flew open, I jumped. Swinging my head around, I promptly choked on my tea when I saw who was standing there.

It was Gabriella. Her long pale hair was pulled up in a ponytail, she wore leggings and a loose t-shirt. She had a very unhappy Danielle on her hip, and my sister's face appeared to be five shades of green. "Me and you?" she practically growled. "Estella, we need to talk."

Horrified, I jumped to my feet. "What are you doing here? Are you *insane*?"

"No, I'm not insane," she said from between her teeth, "but I might throw up on you."

"Lala!" Danielle saw me and reached out.

I took Danielle, and immediately pulled Gabriella inside. She melted into the nearest chair.

"You should probably get a bucket..." she warned

me.

Her words had me scrambling for the mop bucket Amanda kept in the laundry room. I slid it under her. "Jesus H Christ!" I swore. "You have no business being up and out of bed."

Gabriella was ignoring my lecture and was breathing hard. She started to heave. "Oh god," she moaned, and pitched forward in the chair.

I grabbed her shoulder to steady her. "Don't you dare pass out! If you do so help me god, Gabriella, I will call 911."

Fortunately for me, she didn't pass out or throw up. Gabriella grabbed the bucket, dry heaved a few times, and finally belched. I patted her shoulder and tried to get her to slow her breathing down. Dashing to the sink, I soaked a clean dish towel in cold water, wrung it out, and draped it across the back of her neck. After a few minutes, she shuddered and slowly raised herself upright, resting her back against the chair.

Crisis averted, I got a can of ginger ale out of the fridge and popped the top. "Sip on this." I passed it to her and placed Danielle on the floor. Snagging a wooden spoon out of the crock on Amanda's counter, I passed it to the toddler, and she began happily whacking the floor with it.

"Thanks." Gabriella left the bucket in her lap as she sipped at the soda.

"What were you thinking?" I asked my sister.

"I was thinking, I needed to talk to you, and since

you weren't answering your phone—"

"My phone died," I said, sitting in the kitchen chair next to her.

"Well Chauncey finally told us this morning where you were, and I was feeling better, so I loaded Danielle in the car and drove—"

"*Madre de dios*! You drove here?"

"No, I flew on my broom," she snapped. "Stop interrupting me, damn it."

"Sorry." I tried not to smile. It was so good to see my sister acting more like her usual self.

"Just so we're clear, neither Philippe or I had any idea what Camilla was cooking up. Secondly, you were never a burden on us. You have been a lifeline. We both love you. I don't know how we'd have ever managed the past few weeks without your help. You will *always* have a place in our home. No matter what. Do you understand?" The volume of her voice went up on the last three words.

"I—"

She cut me off with a gesture. "I said: *do you understand*?"

"Yes." I nodded meekly, hoping to get her to calm down. "Yes, Gabriella, I understand."

Gabriella wiped the cool cloth across her brow. "I finally heard about everything that happened, and I'm beyond sorry that there was such a big misunderstanding between you, Camilla, and Gran."

"There wasn't a misunderstanding." I crossed my

arms. "Camilla is taking over the farmhouse; she sent Gran to tell me I can't move back."

"Camilla is a hormone with feet." Gabriella exhaled noisily and set the bucket on the floor. "By the goddess, she hasn't had a clear thought in her head since she figured out she was pregnant. She and I exchanged words over this, and she's devastated at how it all turned out."

I didn't answer because I didn't give a damn whether or not Camilla was upset. Danielle stood up and toddled over to me. She lifted her arms and I picked her up and tucked her on my lap. I dropped a kiss to my niece's head. "I missed you, *mija*."

"My Lala," Danielle said, patting my hand with her own.

"Now," Gabriella began, "the truth is that Philippe and I were planning to have you move into our old bedroom, so you would have some privacy and your own ensuite bathroom."

"Wait. What?"

"Estella, we've had this in the works from the beginning. I have all these things ordered for your room: new drapes, linens, décor...It's been arriving for the past couple of weeks."

"I never saw any new décor or drapes and stuff," I said, confused.

"That's because we've been stashing it all at Chauncey's place, so you wouldn't see it," she explained. "Your new room re-do was going to be a big surprise. Philippe and I wanted to make it special for you, and then this fiasco with Camilla happened."

I studied her carefully. Gabriella was still pale, but she looked better, and more importantly, I knew that she was telling me the truth. I could hear it in her voice.

"I believe you," I said.

Gabriella nodded and drained the last of the ginger ale from the can. "Well, that's something anyway."

"Can I get you anything else, Gabriella?"

"Ice cream?" she said hopefully.

I chuckled. "You craving fudgesicles again?"

Gabriella covered her mouth to muffle a burp. "Always."

I reached for her free hand. "I'm glad you came to see me today. Even though I still think you should be lying down with your feet up."

"I'm supposed to be avoiding stress too." Gabriella pressed the back of her hand to her forehead. "I hope my blood pressure doesn't go all crazy from this," she said theatrically, slanting a look over at me to see my reaction.

"Well played." I patted her arm and tried not to laugh.

She grinned and laid her hands over her baby bump. "I'm a delicate little flower, I'll have you know."

I burst out laughing. "Delicate, my ass."

She reached for my hand. "I love you, Estella."

"Aw, hell," I grumbled. "Don't get all sappy."

"Can't help it," she said, giving my hand a squeeze.

My new phone began to ring. Obviously, it was Chauncey; no one else had my new number yet.

I picked it up and hit accept. "Hey, Chauncey."

"No one can find Gabriella or Danielle!" His voice was panicked.

"Calm down, Chauncey," I said. "They're both right here with me, at Amanda's house."

"Oh, thank god," he breathed. "Wait. Do you mean that she drove there?"

"Well," I said, "she didn't fly down to the village on her broom. The baby's car seat won't fit."

Gabriella snorted with laughter.

I heard Chauncey speak to someone. Obviously Philippe, because I heard very loud and angry French words being shouted.

"Stay there. All of you," Chauncey ordered. "We're coming."

"Oh, for Christ's sake, Marquette," I said. "Tone down the machismo. We're perfectly fine—"

"Stay put!" he cut me off and ended the call.

"Well," I said to my sister. "It would seem that the Marquette men are on their way. Coming to collect their wayward women."

"Oh, for fuck's sake." Gabriella rolled her eyes.

"Ha!" Danielle chimed in.

"Philippe sounded pretty pissed off," I warned her, placing my phone back on the table. "I could hear him in the background."

"Was he swearing in French?" my sister wanted to

145

know.

"He was."

Gabriella crossed her arms over her chest. "I don't suppose you could make another tree fall over the road and buy us a bit more time?"

I did a double take. "I didn't have anything to do with that tree. It was the storm."

Gabriella smiled. "Estella, I felt the magick. It was angry and it left a trail through the ether."

"I don't even know what that means," I said. "But that magick *wasn't* mine. At least, I don't think it was."

"Umm hmm." Gabriella smiled. "We'll work on you having better control after you move back home with us."

"No way, it couldn't have been me. I wouldn't even know how to..." I trailed off when two dishes of ice cream appeared on the table in front of each of us. A second later and spoons materialized beside the bowls

"Oh my goddess. *Chocolate*." Gabriella pounced. "Normally I'd ask where it came from, but I know the spirit of Amanda's house has a mind of its own."

I picked up my own spoon. "I'd say it likes you. It let you right in, and even gave you your favorite ice cream."

"I love this old house." Gabriella scooped up a spoonful, tasted it, and sighed. "Thank you, house."

In response the kitchen lights pulsed three times.

Danielle giggled at the light show.

I shared my ice cream with Danielle and tried not to

react as Gabriella enthusiastically plowed her way through the scoops of ice cream in her bowl.

"The twins are hungry," she said around a mouthful.

"I'm not judging," I said soberly.

***

After Philippe rounded up his wife and daughter and Chauncey drove Gabriella's car back to the mansion, I scrubbed and mopped the kitchen to thank Amanda for her hospitality.

I also cleaned the guest room that I'd stayed in, and its adjoining bath too. I changed out the bed sheets and washed all the towels and linens I'd used while I'd been there, so it was as good as new. I was folding the last of the towels when Amanda returned home. She fussed at me, insisting that it wasn't necessary, but I thought it was the least I could do.

Chauncey came and picked me up later that evening, and upon my return to the family wing of the mansion, I found that all of my belongings had already been moved into the former primary suite. Chauncey explained that he'd carried over the boxes of new linens and accessories that Gabriella had ordered for me earlier in the day.

Chauncey gave me a one-armed hug and left. Philippe gathered up Danielle, with a warning to Gabriella not to lift anything heavy, and he went out too. My sister sat in a club chair with a smile, pointed out the new mattress set and the soft cotton sheets that were already on the bed, and then told me to start opening boxes.

To my delight, the first box I opened revealed a midnight blue comforter and pillow shams with celestial designs scattered across it all. There were golden moons, suns, and stars on the fabric, and Gabriella had also found star-shaped blue velvet throw pillows too.

"Stars for Estella seemed pretty appropriate," she said. "Wait until you see the bathroom."

"Gabriella, this is too much..."

"Go and look at the bathroom," she said with a big smile.

I went to the bathroom door and opened it. It had originally been done in all white, with a snowy vanity, white subway tile and chrome fixtures, and the floor was done in a vintage looking white hexagon tile. While all the tile had remained the same, the room still appeared amazingly different. The large double vanity had been painted a striking navy blue. Modern, gold-toned drawer pulls and a faucet had been installed, and there were dark blue towels trimmed in starry fabric hanging from the gold-toned towel racks.

"Wow!" I said.

Gabriella came up behind me to peer over my shoulder. "I told you. I've been planning this for weeks. The crew wasn't only doing the attic reno. They refreshed the bathroom and repainted the bedroom too."

"Thank you," I said. "It's the prettiest bathroom I've ever seen."

"I'm so happy you like it," she said.

"It's amazing. Very magickal." I gave her a hug. "Let's get you off your feet, *mamacita*."

"Sheesh, you nag as much as Philippe."

"Yeah, yeah." I steered her back towards a leather club chair in the bedroom. "My ears are still ringing over the top-volume lecture you got when he showed up at Amanda's."

Gabriella waved that off. "Oh, I let him shout and fuss over me from time to time. It gives him the illusion that he's in control."

"Now that you mention it," I said, "I had noticed that you were acting suitably chastised as he lectured you."

"And *I* noticed that you were biting your lip, trying not to laugh."

"The almost-tears were a nice touch," I said dryly.

"They were, weren't they?" Gabriella grinned and pointed to another box. "Open that one next."

I ripped open the packing tape and found a woven throw, also done in a celestial motif in blue, cream, and gold.

"I thought that would look good draped over one of the club chairs." Gabriella pointed to the one she was sitting in.

I held it out to her. "Go ahead. Do all the fluffing you want, but sit down and take breaks every once in a while, will ya?"

"Deal!" Gabriella rose to her feet and started to add the finishing touches.

We put the bedspread on together and slipped the pillows inside the shams. While I added the throw pillows to the bed, she placed a huge chunk of crystal on the dresser. Next, Gabriella artfully arranged the throw over one of the chairs. I had to admit, it did look nice. My sister was in her element, and it made her so happy that I stood back and let her putter.

She pointed out to me that the club chairs could swivel and face the French doors to the balcony. "On fall nights you can sit here and feel the breeze come off the cliffs."

"That sounds nice," I said agreeably. "Hey Gabriella, Leroy had lent me some paranormal investigative equipment. Did you pack that up or is it still in the nursery?"

"I wasn't sure what that was for, so I left it in place."

"Good." I nodded.

I'd already decided, out of an abundance of caution, that I would keep those doors to the balcony locked. There'd been no sign of Victoria. Not since Amanda and I had warded the mansion a couple of weeks ago, but better safe than sorry.

Gabriella finally decided everything was suitably in place and left me to settle in. I heard her move off down the hall to the tower room where Philippe was with Danielle. Taking a moment for myself, I studied my new room with pleasure. It was moody, magickal and romantic.

My new cell phone buzzed in my pocket. I pulled it out and checked the screen. No surprise, it was Chauncey calling.

I hit accept. "Hey, hot stuff," I said by way of greeting.

"Did you get all settled in?" he asked.

"I did," I said. "It's a very pretty room."

"We had a hell of a time trying to keep all those boxes hidden from you."

"I don't suppose you'd like to come over here and check out the space with me? We could break in the mattress."

"That wouldn't be very discreet," he said.

I smiled. "Oh, I bet I could figure out a way to smuggle you in here."

He chuckled. "I was thinking the same, but it wouldn't be respectful to Gabriella and Philippe."

"Respectful?" I asked.

"Well, the nursery is right next to your room," he pointed out.

I gasped. "Dear god no! I bet they *never* had sex in this room before...Oh wait. Yes, they have; hence the twins."

"Why don't we plan on getting together for dinner, tomorrow evening," he suggested. "My shift ends at six. You could come over here, and we'd be alone."

"I like the sound of that," I said. "You're not gonna make pasta again, are you?"

"Maybe I'll surprise you," he said.

"If you're ordering pizza, make that extra cheese, mushrooms and no onions."

He chuckled. "I'll have something delivered."

"Good night, Chauncey."

"Good night, Estella."

We disconnected and I went to go join my family. It felt good to be back, almost as if I truly belonged after all.

CHAPTER TEN

The second night after I moved back to the mansion, Philippe, Gabriella, and Danielle were all tucked up in the tower room when I told them—very casually—that I was going over to have dinner with Chauncey. My announcement had Gabriella grinning.

"I *knew* it!" she said. "There were definite vibes coming off you two the other day! How long have you two been seeing each other?"

I shrugged and struggled against embarrassment. "Technically, I see him almost every day since I moved here. Because, you know, he *works* here on the other side of the mansion."

Philippe laid a hand on Gabriella's arm. "*Ma belle.*"

"What?" Gabriella frowned at her husband. "The next words out of your mouth better not be 'to stay out of it.'"

Philippe sent her a look, and next shifted his attention to me. "Have a nice evening, Estella."

"Er, thanks, Philippe." It was everything I had to

stand there while Gabriella grinned, and Philippe looked uncomfortable.

"Want me to help you pick out something nice to wear to dinner?" my sister offered.

"Ah, no," I said. "I'm only going over to his place. It's casual."

Gabriella smiled.

"It's no big deal. We are only..." I shut up the moment I realized how stupid I sounded.

Suddenly feeling awkward, I shuffled down the hall to my new room. Despite what I'd told Gabriella, I went to the closet and pulled open the door. I gave serious consideration to changing into a nicer outfit. I did have a couple of dresses, but that was a bit too obvious.

If I showed up in a dress and heels that'd be completely out of character, and he'd know something was up. Better to keep things light, playful even, and let him become more comfortable with me and hopefully return my feelings.

Squaring my shoulders, I left my jeans, sneakers, and a chambray shirt as they were. I did detour into my bathroom and freshened up my face. I knew how to bump up the package a bit. I deepened my eye shadow, went ahead and added a muted plum lipstick, and gave my hair a quick tousle.

Satisfied with my appearance, I went down the stairs, out the family entrance, and walked around the house heading for Chauncey's apartment.

Jogging up the stairs of the old coach house, I knocked on his door.

He opened the door and smiled. "Estella."

"Hey. How was your day?" I asked.

"Busy. Please come in," he said, holding open the door. "I ordered dinner. It will be delivered in about an hour."

I stepped inside and smiled. "An hour you say?"

"Yes."

I cast my eyes over him. He looked mighty fine in his dark suit. His tie was off and a few buttons were undone, but he'd hadn't taken the jacket off yet. *Oh, yeah,* I thought, *he's all mine tonight.* I suddenly had an urge to tear the clothes right off of him.

"I can make us some appetizers if you like," he offered and shut the door.

"No, thanks," I said, stepping up so I was right in his face. "The only appetizer I want is you."

His eyebrows rose. "Is that right?"

"It is." I yanked him forward by his lapels. Our bodies slammed together, and it gave me a nice solid jolt all the way to my toes. "I thought I'd start at your neck..." I leaned closer and kissed his throat. "Nibble my way down." I scraped my teeth across his nape. "Interested?" I asked.

His hands had settled on my hips, and now they gripped them. He said my name once before dropping his mouth to mine and kissing me deeply.

In response, I tried to unbutton his shirt, but the

buttons eluded me. Frustrated with it, I yanked, and the buttons went flying. I shoved the jacket from his shoulders and his shirt was soon to follow.

He returned the favor, and I shivered when I felt my old chambray shirt tear as he pulled it from me. Soon all of our clothes had been tugged off and thrown around the room. We made it as far as the couch before we lowered ourselves down to it and promptly went crazy over each other. The orgasm hit hard and fast for the both of us, and afterwards Chauncey dropped his forehead to mine and tried to catch his breath.

"Wow." I patted his butt. "That was fun."

"Fun?" he lifted his head to gaze at me dolefully.

"Yes, fun."

He said nothing in reply, yet stared at me so intently, that I wondered if I'd insulted him.

"Fun," I repeated. "You know, like the way you and I went crazy on the counter in Amanda's kitchen." I gave a happy sigh. "That counter was exactly the right height for you to stand while I wrapped my—"

He cut me off with a kiss.

I narrowed my eyes at him when he let me up for air. "Are you're embarrassed about that?"

"No," he said. "I still can't believe we did that."

"Relax," I said. "I disinfected the spot on the counter that we defiled, after you left."

His face went red at the word *defiled*.

I grinned at him. "You're so cute when you're flustered."

"I am not flustered," he said. "More like amazed that I wanted you so badly that I didn't care about where we were."

"Aww." I gave his nose a kiss. "You're more old-fashioned than I thought. It's ruining your playboy image, Chauncey."

"I was never a playboy," he grumbled.

"Baby, I saw those old social media posts. You partied it up in every rich playground of Europe."

"I think you are confusing social media posts with real life."

"You gonna try and tell me that back in your old glory days, when you were bopping around with the racing set, that you never cut loose and went wild?"

"No, I did not."

I ran my fingers through his hair, smoothing it back from his face. "You telling me that you've never had spontaneous sex someplace inappropriate before?"

"Absolutely not," he said.

"No nookie in the backseat of a limo with a supermodel?"

He raised his eyebrows. "I'd never."

"You never did it on the open deck of a fancy yacht while you were cruising the Mediterranean?"

"Ah, no," he said. "There's nothing sexy about a sunburnt back-side."

I worked hard to keep a straight face. "Well, I'm glad you kept your back-side protected from those damaging UV rays. Because, you do have a great ass," I said, giving it a friendly squeeze.

Chauncey began to laugh. "Estella, only you would say that to me."

"What?" I frowned. "You do have a nice ass. Hasn't anyone ever complimented you before?"

"Er...not in quite that way," he admitted and rose to his feet.

I sat up halfway and rested back on my elbows. "Baby, it's a good thing you quit hanging around with all those uptight society types."

"I've put that all well behind me," he said, bending over to retrieve our clothes from the floor.

I watched him straighten things, folding our discarded clothes, and found it adorable. When he asked me if I'd like a shower, I followed him into the small bathroom. He got the water going and I eyeballed the standard bathtub and shower curtain set up.

"No way we're going for round two in there."

He startled and glanced at me warily from over his shoulder. "I wasn't planning on trying to christen the shower this evening."

Deliberately, I shrugged. "Well yeah, I figure with that old racing injury of yours, sex in the shower wouldn't be smart anyway."

"Is that a dare?" he asked, sounding slightly offended.

"Nope. Safety is important. You know, most home accidental fatalities occur in the bathroom." I bit back a smile as he gaped at me. "Besides, I'm looking forward to that pizza," I said, stepping in the tub. "I'd like to be alive to enjoy it."

"I think that we can survive bathing together," he said and joined me.

"I'm game if you are," I said, tossing a bar of soap to him.

***

He did better than ordering pizza. Chauncey had ordered a couple of steaks, with potatoes and a salad. He poured us some of the *Trois Amis* wine and we ended up seated at his small kitchen table and eating our meal. He in sweatpants and a t-shirt, and me in my jeans and a borrowed shirt from him. My chambray shirt hadn't survived him pulling it off me.

"Sorry about your shirt," he said as we ate supper.

I shrugged. "I'm not."

"Still, I should have taken more care."

I had been reaching for my wine glass and now I stopped. "More care? What are you talking about?"

Chauncey took a sip of his wine. "Tonight and yesterday, I wanted you too badly to...I should have been more considerate, and careful with you."

"Do you hear me complaining?" I asked.

He simply stared at me.

"Are you unhappy with the way we have sex?" I asked flatly.

"Not at all," he said instantly. "I've never had a lover

who both thrilled me *and* made me laugh. I only meant that, considering...your background and experience, that I wasn't as gentle or as thoughtful as I could have been."

I frowned. "I'm going to have to ask you to clarify what you meant by *my background and experience*."

"I was concerned that I might inadvertently trigger you, while we made love."

"What?" I sat there dumbfounded. I didn't know what else to say.

"You made it clear that you had experienced sexual violence in the past. The first time I kissed you, you warned me that you don't like hands near your face. Which is why I have never touched your face or even your hair without asking permission first."

It hit me suddenly that he was right. He had always asked first. But instead of making me feel better, it made my stomach turn. "You think I'm damaged goods, is that it?"

"No," he said patiently. "You explained that you had fought hard to keep yourself safe. I was only trying to be understanding and respectful."

"So, you felt sorry for me?" I set my wine glass down very carefully. "What has all this been over the past few days, pity sex?"

His eyes flashed hot with temper. "Don't you *ever* say that. Not ever again." His tone was harsh, clipped, and furious. "You know better."

"You just apologized for *not* being considerate the

last two times we had sex," I said hotly. "And here I sat like a dumb-ass thinking: damn that bout in the kitchen and us ripping the clothes off each other a bit ago was totally hot and amazing... Only to hear that you're embarrassed by it."

"I was not embarrassed by it, and please don't refer to us making love as a *bout*."

"Excuse me?"

"I said—"

"Oh I heard you, Chauncey. I was so shocked that those words came out of your mouth that it was an automatic response."

"Estella, you and I—" he began.

"So let me get this straight." I spoke right over him. "You are uncomfortable with me being the instigator?"

He dropped his head in his hands. Slowly, he lifted his head and stared me straight in the eye. "I am going to speak and you are going to listen. If you interrupt me, I swear to god I will gag you."

"Gag me?" I repeated. "Try that and I'll kick your ass from here to next week."

"Estella." His voice was flat. "Do not push me."

I crossed my arms and sat back in my chair.

"I happily allowed you to take the lead," he said, "as I was concerned that otherwise I might inadvertently bring back a bad memory. That does *not* mean that I did not enjoy myself or that I was dissatisfied with our love making. What it means is that I am trying to go slowly, to be attentive, and to take my cues from you." He blew out a long breath. "And I'm doing all of this, trying to be careful of your feelings, because I've fallen in love with you."

We sat in humming silence for a few moments. My mouth had gone bone dry. Picking up my wine, I took a sip before I spoke.

"You love me?" I finally managed to ask.

"Yes," he said simply.

My hands started to shake. I set the glass down before I spilled it. "When?" I asked. "When did you fall in love with me?"

"When?" He ran his finger over his jaw as he considered the question. "You know, I can't look back and say exactly when it happened. It was sort of an irresistible attraction. First, I was awestruck seeing the security video of how you handled those bullies who tried to beat up Brooke. Then at the hotel's grand opening last year, you came to Amanda's defense, and knocked out a drunk with a swift uppercut and all I could think was: *Dear god, what a woman*!"

"Aww," I said with a chuckle.

He smiled gently at me, reached for my hand, and held it. "After Pierre-Michel and Victoria used us—"

"Yeah, that was awkward discovering I was kissing you while someone else had control of my body—our bodies," I corrected myself.

"Awkward and frustrating," Chauncey agreed. "Afterward, I couldn't get you out of my mind. For a while I tried to convince myself that my attraction to you was only because *his* memories were twisted up in my own impressions, but I knew that wasn't the case."

"That possession thing messed with my head too," I said.

"Yet we still remained friends," he said. "And although your friendship has become one of the most important in my life, I found myself wanting so much more. Your courage amazed me. You dove in and took on a ghost to try and save me when I was possessed a second time. You literally caught me when I dropped out of the air."

"Well." I reached up and patted his face. "I'd never let you fall without trying to catch you. You're too pretty to bash that face up."

"I'm not pretty."

"Yes, you are," I argued. "Don't go fishing for compliments, Chauncey. We both know you're gorgeous."

"You're the one who is gorgeous," he said with a smile.

"Nah." I shook my head. "I'm too curvy."

"Your curves make me crazy. I thought I'd proven that to you. Perhaps another demonstration is in order..."

"A demonstration?' I smiled slowly. "Tell me more."

"Estella," he said. "Don't interrupt me when I'm giving you compliments. You're getting me off track."

"Sorry."

"As I was saying," he continued, "I was touched by

your generosity when you offered to help out Philippe and Gabriella. You dove right in and took care of Danielle—"

"Well," I said. "I love that little monster."

"Stop interrupting," he said. "I'm trying to tell you when I realized I loved you and there's so many instances. You were physically attacked by an insane ghost at the mansion and yet you still went back to help keep your family safe. I've said it before, and I hope *this* time you will listen to me. You are the bravest woman I have ever known, Estella. I only hope to be worthy of you."

Tears welled up. "Damn it, don't make me cry."

"I love you." He reached for my hand and held it.

"Okay, my turn," I said, linking fingers with him. "You've always been there at the edges of my mind. From the first day we met until today. You're the first thing I think of each morning, and my last thought at night—even when I am annoyed with you. When you showed up at Amanda's looking for me the other day, I knew one hundred percent that I loved you, and I thought maybe if we became lovers that you'd fall for me, the real me, and love me despite it all."

"I didn't fall in love with you because we had sex," he said gently. "I fell in love with you because of who you are." He started to reach up for my hair and stopped himself.

"You don't have to ask permission to touch my face or hair anymore," I said. "If you want to touch me, go ahead. In fact, you can pretty much do whatever you like with me—that is as long as I'm into it too."

"Come over here," he said, pointing at his lap.

I stood and went to him, sliding on his lap. I looped my arm around him and pressed my cheek against his shoulder. "I love you too, Chauncey," I said quietly.

"I love you, Estella," he said, wrapping his arms around me. I held him tight as emotions swirled through me. He pressed a kiss to my hair, and I squeezed my eyes shut, trying not to cry. It was a wonderful moment; damned if I'd cry my way though it.

"I'm not especially good at all this emotional stuff, Chauncey," I said. "I don't want to screw it up. I've never been in love before. It's scary."

"Me neither," he said. "We can learn together."

"Deal," I said.

We sat like that, simply holding each other, as the food went cold on the table. I don't think either of us cared.

I tipped my face up to his and we kissed. It was slow, deep, and hot. He ran his hands all over me and eventually wrapped his fingers in my hair. After a while, he lifted his mouth from mine. "I'm taking you to bed." His voice was low and husky.

"I won't argue with that," I said.

"I love you." He stood with me in his arms. "Let me show you how much."

***

I spent the night at his apartment. His alarm woke me up the next morning and I bounded out of bed and hurried to get dressed and back to the mansion to help with Danielle and breakfast. I couldn't find my bra and instead of wasting time looking for it, I tugged his shirt on and zipped up my jeans.

Chauncey sat up with a yawn. "What's the rush?"

"I have to go. Danielle will be waking soon."

"Oh, I see," he said. "I tell you that I love you, spend all night showing you how much—"

"Very creatively too, I might add," I said, cramming my feet down in my shoes.

"Why, thank you." He nodded.

"No, thank *you*." I grinned and sat on the side of the bed to tie my shoelaces.

His hands roamed over my back and headed around, straight for my chest.

"You're not wearing a bra," he said.

I gave him a quick kiss. "Nope. Couldn't find it."

"Come back to bed, Estella."

I stood and eyeballed him. He lay there all rumpled and sexy with the sheet pooled low at his hips. "God damn it," I swore half-heartedly. "I really do have to leave."

He started to rise from the bed and warily I took off for the front door.

"Afraid I'll persuade you to stay?" he called after me.

"You know you could." I blew him a kiss and let myself out.

I ran around the eastern wing of the mansion and entered in the code for the family entrance. I jogged up the stairs and congratulated myself when I peeked in the nursery and saw that Danielle was still asleep.

I zipped into my room, put on fresh clothes, and fixed my face. I was brushing my hair into a high ponytail when I heard Danielle stirring over the nursery monitor. With a smile, I headed to her room to get her changed and ready for the day.

I stuck to my routine, and after breakfast I took Danielle out to the gardens. Puffy clouds were gathering in the October sky and the temperatures were mild. I admired how the leaves were beginning to change on the trees and figured I probably had a goofy smile on my face. In fact, I hadn't stop smiling since Chauncey had told me that he loved me.

Danielle wasn't interested in chasing the ball that I rolled to her; instead she was more fascinated in scalping whatever flower that was growing along the garden path.

"Your mother will kill me," I said and scooped Danielle up, taking her to the grassy area. I chased her around for awhile. After she was bored with that, I put her in the baby swing.

"Estella!"

I turned to look and saw Drusilla. She was walking toward me and held Alex and Abby's hands in hers.

I felt my smile fade. Blowing out a breath, I psyched myself up for a confrontation. Hopefully with the kids present it wouldn't be bad.

"Hey, Dru," I said as she came closer.

Danielle saw the kids and wanted down. I unstrapped her from the baby swing and lifted her out. As soon as her feet hit the ground, she was off, chasing the other kids across the lawn.

Dru dropped down to the grass in the shade and patted the spot beside her. "Let's talk," she said.

"I don't want to argue with you, Dru," I said.

She reached up, grabbed my hand, and gave me a tug. "That works out nicely. I don't want to argue with you either."

With a sigh, I rolled my eyes and sat next to her on the grass.

"I'm sorry that I was unaware of everything that went down between you, Cammy and Gran," she said.

Don't trust her. The voice slithered into my mind. *They'll use you and take away everything you love...*

My heart rate picked up, and I felt trapped and afraid.

You should be afraid.

I bore down and pushed my way through my unease. I was *not* afraid of Drusilla. That was ridiculous. I tuned back into her as she continued to speak.

"Still," she said, "me being busy with the kids is no excuse."

"You had your hands more than full with Alex and

Abby," I said. "I'm not upset with you, Drusilla."

"Camilla is making herself sick worrying about it all. She's convinced that you hate her."

I couldn't think of how to best answer her. So, I kept my mouth shut.

You can't trust your sister. She wants everything you have. She's covetous and will do whatever she can to take it away, and then she'll destroy you...

"Covetous?" I said out loud.

"What did you say?" Dru asked.

"Who's that?" Abby had stopped a few feet in front of us and stood pointing.

Drusilla turned to look. "Who are you pointing at, sweetheart?"

"The lady," Abby said.

"What lady?" I asked, rising to my feet and looking around. I saw nothing except trees, the flower beds and the kids playing on the grass.

"Where do you see the lady, Abby?" Drusilla stood as well.

"Right there." Abby pointed towards the children.

I spun and saw that Alex was looking up at something, while Danielle was huddled close behind him.

"Look at them," Dru whispered. "Standing so still. Something is wrong."

The light changed and the sun went behind the clouds. It was then that I saw the faintest shimmer on the air. There was something taking shape out there on the grass in front of Alex and Danielle.

"Don't you see the lady, Mama?" Abby said to Drusilla

Children are a joy, are they not? that voice whispered in my ear.

And at that moment it hit me. That sly familiar voice...I'd heard it before on the third-floor balcony. First, when she tried to push me over the railing. More recently, when she'd successfully invaded my mind, used my deepest fears against me, and sent me running from the mansion.

"Damn it," I muttered. "The bitch played me."

CHAPTER ELEVEN

"What lady, Abby?" Dru desperately asked her daughter.

"She's right there. She's wearing a yellow dress," Abby insisted.

Abby's words had my heart slamming hard against my ribs. The spirit of Victoria Midnight typically manifested wearing a yellow dress. My worst fears confirmed, I bolted toward the children. "Alex! Danielle!" I shouted.

"What is it?" Drusilla yelled. "What's happening?"

The shadows deepened and now I could make out a shape. A woman in a long dress, with flowing hair. She was positioned maybe two feet in front of the children, and she was reaching out her hand toward Alex. Behind me I heard more shouting, but I didn't bother looking. Instead, I kept moving, trying to get to the children as quickly as I could.

"Don't you touch them!" I yelled at Victoria's ghost.

I pounded across the lawn, and as I rushed closer to

Alex and Danielle, I felt the frigid cold. It was a horrible slap to the senses on what should have been a pretty October afternoon. Still, I didn't break stride, I just dove headfirst, wrapped my arms around both of the kids and rolled with them over the grass and away from the cold spot.

Tucking the kid's heads in tight against my chest, I let the momentum carry us farther away from where the spirit had manifested. I shut my eyes as we tumbled, rolling several times, and by the time we came to a stop, Alex was crying, and Danielle was wailing for all she was worth.

"Estella!" Drusilla shouted my name as she raced in, a few seconds behind me.

I opened my eyes and saw nothing menacing. Better yet, I felt no more of that unearthly cold. Slowly, I sat up. "I got you," I said to the children. "It's going to be okay."

But they weren't okay. Alex's teeth were chattering, and Danielle was shivering.

Drusilla skidded to a stop on the grass. She had run behind me, carrying Abby. "What the hell was that thing?" she asked, setting Abby on her feet.

"Mama!" Alex cried, reaching for Dru.

"Alex!" Drusilla gasped. "He's so cold," she said, taking him in her arms. "Oh, sweetie," she crooned, holding him as he cried.

Suddenly Philippe and Chauncey were there too. Philippe reached down and picked up his daughter. He tucked Danielle against his chest. "Danielle's skin is like ice. She's shivering."

"That's because they were too close to a spirit," I said.

"Spirit?" Dru gaped at me. "Oh god. A lady in yellow. Was that Victoria?"

"Yes," I said as Chauncey helped me to my feet. "She's been hanging around the mansion."

"*What?*" Philippe and Drusilla said at the same time.

I brushed grass from my jeans. "She's been picking on me for a while. I banished her from the house with Amanda's help, but I guess she's still haunting the grounds."

"Picking on you?" Drusilla said.

"It's a long story," I told her.

Chauncey took my arm. "You're bleeding, Estella," he said.

I glanced down and saw that both of my elbows were skinned up. "I'm fine."

"Let's take the children inside," Philippe suggested.

"We should call Amanda," Chauncey said.

"Immediately," Philippe agreed.

Abby stood there, her brown eyes much too big in her face. I hunkered down and held out my arms to her. "Come here, Abby," I said.

She walked to me. "Aunt Estella," she said, laying her head on my shoulder.

"You were so brave," I said, hugging the little girl.

"I don't like that lady," Abby said. "Is she all gone?"

"She is for now," I said, hoping it was true. "You were super smart to tell your mom that you saw a stranger. You knew something was wrong before anyone else did."

"I'm not in trouble?" she asked timidly.

"No, you're not in trouble!" I said. "You did a great job protecting your brother and cousin."

"I'm so proud of you, Abby," Drusilla told her daughter.

"How about a piggy-back ride?" I turned so she could climb up and Abby happily leapt on my back. I stood, gave her a small bounce and started walking.

"You went flying through the air!" Abby hugged my neck. "You rolled over the grass so fast with Alex and the baby."

"And took about five years off my life," Chauncey said, resting his hand on my lower back as we walked together. "Are you certain you are all right?"

"Yeah, a couple of scraped elbows are no big deal," I said as we fell in step behind Dru and Philippe.

Chauncey reached over and pressed a kiss to my cheek as we walked together. Abby tilted her head at that, not quite sure what to make of it.

In response, I boosted Abby higher in the air making her laugh again.

"Do you want me to carry her?" Chauncey offered.

"Nah, I got her," I said. "Would you call Amanda for me? Like right now and let her know what's happened? I bet she'll know what to do for the kids."

"I will," Chauncey said, pulling his cell phone from his pocket.

"Miss Amanda is the librarian," Abby said. "We get our books from her."

"Umm hmm," I agreed. "Amanda is super smart, that's why we're calling her."

"Okay." Abby hugged me tighter.

"Don't worry, *mija*," I said to Abby. "It's going to be fine."

"I'm not scared," Abby said. "Mama says the daughters of Midnight stick together."

"You betcha," I said. "Nobody messes with our family. Right, Abby?"

"Right!" she laughed.

***

Alex and Danielle warmed up quickly enough. Their mothers put them in a warm bath and Gabriella surrounded the edges of the tub with healing crystals. In no time at all, two-year-old Alex and eighteen-month-old Danielle were giggling, splashing and playing in the tub like old friends.

Garrett came immediately from the winery when he heard the news, and now Gabriella, Philippe, Garrett and Drusilla, and Chauncey were all having a confab in the tower room. Abby seemed fine and the younger children were playing together on the carpet. I excused myself from the group and stood downstairs waiting for

Amanda in the lobby at the eastern entrance.

"Never a dull moment," she said by way of greeting.

I gave her a one-armed hug. "Glad you are here."

"Tell me what you saw and felt," Amanda said. "I want your impressions before anyone else's."

I nodded and explained what had happened.

"Abby spotted her first?" Amanda thought that over. "I've always said that children are more sensitive to the unseen than most adults would ever imagine."

"The kids were ice cold when I reached them," I said. "It scared the hell out of me, I don't mind telling you. If that bat-shit crazy ghost wants to mess with me, that's fine. But she threatened the kids' safety, Amanda. They're only babies."

Amanda pursed her lips as she thought it over. "Victoria's spirit is ramping up. She's not acting the sweet ghost or the tragic victim any longer."

"No, she's not," I said. "She's let her crazy out to play, and so help me I will do my best to banish that ghost to the nether realms the next chance I get."

Amanda rested her hand on my arm. "You're going to have to tell them about Victoria's attack on you from a few weeks ago. You know that, right?"

I sighed. "Yeah, I know."

Amanda inspected my arm. "What the hell happened to your elbows?"

I shrugged. "I skinned them up when I rolled over the grass with the kids."

"You should tend to them," Amanda said.

"Worried that it'll look bad when I'm wearing my bridesmaid dress next week?" I teased.

"No, I was worried they'd get infected from the dirt and grass."

"I'm going to tend to her injuries personally." Chauncey's voice came from above and behind us.

I turned to find him standing on the landing. He was frowning and holding a first aid kit.

"It's no big deal, Chauncey," I said. "I can take care of it"

"Yeah, yeah...you're *muy macho*," he said. "I'm still going to help you. So just quit your bitchin'."

It was word for word what I'd once said to him, and it made me grin.

"You're just looking for any excuse to get your hands on my body again, admit it," I said, quoting what he'd once said to *me*.

"Guilty," he said, with a wicked grin.

Amanda shook her head at our by-play. "You two slay me."

"Ha!" I nudged her with my elbow. "Guardian. Slaying. Nice pun."

"Come on," Amanda said, and the three of us headed upstairs.

The family went very quiet when Amanda explained that Victoria's M.O. had altered over the past few weeks. "We've documented the change in her behavior," she said. "Victoria's gone from manifesting as sweet and supportive...to a much more menacing figure here at the mansion."

"That's a nice way of saying Victoria is acting bat-shit crazy and mean," I added.

Amanda nodded. "True. The spirit of Victoria Midnight has been exhibiting mentally disturbed and aggressive qualities on more than one occasion."

"Besides her threatening the children, what else has happened?" Philippe asked.

I cleared my throat. "I'm not sure where to begin."

Gabriella whipped her head around and glared at me. "I knew it! Something happened to you. I had the weirdest dreams at the hospital. I kept seeing the balcony railing and the morning glories were weeping. It didn't make any sense."

I winced. "Well, your dreams are right on the money."

"Morning glories are supposed to be protective," Drusilla said.

"I meant to ask you about that," I said to Dru.

Her eyes locked on mine. "And did they protect you?" she asked.

I blew out a breath. "I think they may have helped save my life."

Everyone started speaking at once. They were all firing questions so quickly that I looked to Amanda for help.

Amanda held up her hand for silence. "If you will allow me?" she said. In a way I could only admire, Amanda proceeded to concisely fill the family in on

Victoria's attack on me a few weeks ago.

The family went ballistic at the news.

"I'm fine now," I tried to assure everyone.

"The night it happened," Chauncey said to Philippe, "she stayed awake afterward watching over both you and the baby while you slept. I saw her the next day when she went to Amanda's."

I shrugged. "It's not a big deal. It wasn't like I was going to be able to sleep after all of that anyway."

Chauncey ran his hand down my arm. "Don't brush this off, Estella."

"Estella," Philippe began, "you should have come to me right away!"

Gabriella narrowed her eyes. "You kept this a secret for weeks trying to protect me, didn't you?"

"The last thing you or Philippe needed was more stress," I insisted. "I'm fine. Amanda helped me, and we took care of it. Victoria can't get back inside the house."

Drusilla stood and walked over to Amanda. "You documented it. The attack on Estella. I know you did. I'd like to see the photos please."

"Don't show them to her," I said to Amanda. Which of course, only started another family debate.

While the arguments raged on, Amanda pulled out her cell phone and began tapping the screen. In a moment she had a file pulled up and silently she handed the phone to Drusilla.

Together Garrett and Drusilla studied the images.

Dru actually cringed as she scrolled through them. "Estella, this was serious."

Garrett sent me a look. "It's a damn good thing you're strong. Anyone else she'd have probably pushed over the railing."

"Well, she didn't," I said.

"Let me see!" Gabriella demanded, holding out her hand for the phone.

I could only sigh when Dru handed over the phone to Philippe. Together, he and Gabriella viewed the photos. To my dismay, silent tears began rolling down Gabriella's face.

"Okay, that's enough," I said, easing my sister into a chair. "Let's take it easy, *mamacita*."

"She could have killed you!" Gabriella cried.

"*Pfft.*" I rolled my eyes. "I'm fine, Gabriella. Amanda patched me up, and that very day we came back here and warded the family wing of the mansion, and we also hit the public spaces too."

Gabriella wiped her eyes. "So that's why the paranormal equipment is here."

"Exactly," I said and pulled an ottoman over. "I had Leroy set it up that if any paranormal phenomena started in the nursery, it would set off an alarm." I picked up one of her feet and placed it on the ottoman. "Put your feet up." I placed her other foot beside the first. "Take a breath and calm down."

"Estella." Philippe was beside me, and he surprised me by wrapping me up in his arms. He tucked my head under his chin and held on. "*Petite soeur.*"

"What's that mean?" I asked him.

"Little sister," he said.

"I promise you, I'm fine." I patted his back and he let me go. I stepped back and sent him a smile. "Honestly, Philippe, I'm more worried about the fact that it took me so long to figure out that Victoria has been screwing with my head."

Gabriella glared. "Explain what you mean by that."

I cast a pleading glance at Amanda. She raised one eyebrow in reply. With a quiet sigh, I told the family that I'd recently figured out that Victoria's ghost had been whispering in my ear, or messing with my emotions, trying to make me feel like an outsider and that my sisters were all turning against me.

"Why?" Drusilla asked. "Why would she do that to you?"

"Because she wants me to spring her boyfriend," I said. "She wants me to release the spirit of Pierre-Michel from his portrait, and I refused."

"Before anyone asks," Amanda said, "that portrait is being stored in a safe place. Pierre-Michel's spirit is staying put."

"Considering that I'm his favorite host," Chauncey said, "I am very thankful for that."

Garrett leaned forward. "So can we entrap Victoria's spirit in a similar manner?"

Amanda adjusted her glasses. "To my knowledge, there is no portrait of Victoria Midnight."

"Besides," I argued, "it was Louisa Midnight's evil magick that originally bound Pierre-Michel's spirit to his portrait as punishment for his supposed crimes. And correct me if I'm wrong, but that'd be some pretty intense dark spell-crafting—binding Victoria's spirit to an inanimate object."

"That's exactly right," Amanda said. "We can banish her from the grounds for the short term—but for a lasting solution we need to find a way to encourage her spirit to move on."

"Not easy to do under the best of circumstances," Drusilla said.

"Especially since Victoria is not exactly sane," I pointed out.

"I propose that we do another working to keep Victoria's spirit completely off the Marquette property," Amanda said. "She is already barred from the house, and we can reinforce that. Drusilla, you, Estella, and I will work to keep her presence from the grounds now as well."

"I'm game," Dru said.

"I can help," Gabriella said.

"No!" everyone said at the same time.

"Gabriella," Amanda began, "the magick won't be easy, and considering your pregnancy, I'd prefer that you sit this one out. That goes for Camilla too."

"What about Gran?" Dru asked.

Amanda shook her head. "We know Victoria goes after anyone who is feeling like an outsider. Right now, that's Camilla. It would be best to let Priscilla keep her safe and out of the line of fire at the farmhouse."

"For something like this, you'll need four practitioners," Gabriella pointed out. "One for each direction."

"I *would* feel better with a fourth," Amanda admitted. "One of us holding each cardinal point."

"What about Brooke?" Drusilla asked. "She's powerful when it comes to elemental magick, and I know she'd love to help."

Amanda smiled. "That would work. Are you both comfortable with it?" She looked pointedly at Garrett.

"I say if Brooke wants to help, she certainly can," he said." She'll get out of school in an hour."

"Excellent," Amanda said. "We'll begin at sunset. I have a few things to gather before then. So, I suggest the rest of you go home and rest up. You're going to need all of your energy for the banishing spell."

"I'll speak to Gran," Drusilla said. "Tell her to work protection magick for Camilla and to ward the farmhouse. She can coordinate with us and begin her spells at sunset as well."

"Good idea," Amanda said.

"What about here?" Gabriella asked.

Amanda smiled. "I promise you that this house is sealed up tight. For now, your job is to take care of yourself and those twins."

"I hate being sidelined," Gabriella grumbled.

I patted my sister's head. "I promise, tomorrow I'll

walk you around and show you everything that is in place for the warding."

"Good." Gabriella nodded. "Dru?" she spoke to her older sister. "You better batten down the hatches at your place."

"Planned on it," Dru said with a nod.

Everyone said their goodbyes, and Dru and Garrett took their kids home. Amanda let herself out, and Gabriella and Philippe took the baby upstairs with them to their new suite for a nap. I wasn't surprised. I didn't figure that either one of Danielle's parents would be comfortable letting her out of their sight.

That left Chauncey and I alone together.

"Come with me," he said. Picking up the first aid kit and tucking it under his arm, he reached for my hand.

We walked down the hall together and went straight to my room. He held open the door for me, and after I entered, he shut it and locked it behind us. We went to my bathroom, and I got out a washcloth and scrubbed at my skinned elbows with soap. I patted them dry, and Chauncey put some antibiotic cream on the scrapes and helped me cover the wounds with some oversized bandages.

"Well," I said. "That's all taken care of—"

I didn't get to finish my sentence as he kissed me. With the softest of touches he brushed his hands under my jaw, around to the back of my head, and pulled me close. He continued to kiss me until I thought my brains would leak out of my ears.

Finally, he let me up for air. "It's only a couple of scrapes, Chauncey," I said. "I'm fine."

"Do you have any idea what it did to me to turn the corner of the garden and see you running towards the children?" He pressed his forehead to mine. "I heard you shout, and even though I couldn't see anything, I knew that it had to be bad for you to be moving and diving for them like that."

I took his face in my hands as well. "It was probably the same way I felt seeing you hovering in mid-air while Pierre-Michel yanked you around like a puppet on a string last year."

He exhaled. "For a split second when you grabbed them, the three of you disappeared."

"No shit?"

"No shit," he said in a shaky voice. "Then you were back and rolling across the lawn."

"I didn't say anything to Dru and the others, but I was afraid that Victoria was going to try and take the children with her somehow." I shook my head. "That sounds crazy to say, but after everything I've seen since I moved here, I didn't want to take any chances."

"What happened in the garden...it terrified Philippe," Chauncey admitted. "I've never seen him look that way before."

"He's not the only one that was afraid," I said. "When I realized who that voice belonged to, and Abby said the lady wore a yellow dress, my heart almost stopped."

"I would have never known. I thought you were magnificent."

"*Estella the Magnificent*. Maybe I could get that on a t-shirt." I smiled at the thought. "Could you see Victoria from where you were? I saw the barest of outlines, an impression only, but the cold I felt as I put myself between her and the children was terrifying."

He smoothed my hair away from my face. "I only saw you. Once again risking your own personal safety for those that you love."

I raised my eyebrows. "Would you do any less for those babies?"

He sighed. "No. I'd do anything to keep them safe."

"Then why are you upset with me?" I asked.

"I'm not upset. I love you, Estella." He kissed me again and it was soft and deeply emotional. I felt tears build up behind my eyes. He whispered how much he loved me and when he scooped me up in his arms, and carried me to the bed, he made me feel cherished and safe.

***

At sunset, Amanda, Drusilla, Brooke, and I met in the central spot of the Marquette property. It wasn't too far from the spot where Victoria had manifested earlier in the day. Even after studying magick and working with Amanda for the past year, I was impressed at the amount of energy that the four of us were able to raise.

Drusilla took the north for the earth element. Brooke had west and the element of water. Amanda stood tall in the South for the element of fire, and I held the eastern quarter and called the element of air.

On the grass in the center of our circle, a map of the county rested, with the boundaries of the Marquette property marked on it. Candles in holders were at each cardinal point. A circle of morning glory vines rested on the map, as did protective stones and crystals. Their weight helped keep the map in place. At the height of the ritual, rain began to fall. That was Brooke's contribution, I was sure. She was linked to water deities and magicks after all.

The rainwater coalesced on the map and began to run in a circle, counterclockwise around the edges of the marked area. The flames of the candles jumped and continued to burn straight and true, despite the rain.

Thunder rumbled across the sky, and I saw that Dru's eyes were practically glowing with power. A thin light shone around Amanda, and Brooke's eye were a neon blue. The teen smiled as raindrops seemed to caress her skin. I felt power rush up from the ground and surge through my entire body. My head fell back as the wind suddenly came screaming in from the east. It sent my hair snapping away from my face, and the smell of ozone was heavy in the air.

I felt it the moment the protection spell was sealed around the property lines. It dropped down and met the ground with a force that vibrated through the soles of my feet. Lightning struck a tree at the eastern edge of the property; with a boom and crash, the tree fell. I watched the three other women smile in reaction.

"As we will it..." Amanda intoned.

"So shall it be," we finished together.

The spell was completed, and the elements were thanked and released. Once it was done, the four of us dropped down to the grass. We were exhausted, a little high on the magick we'd called, dripping wet, and laughing like loons.

"That was incredible," I said.

"We rocked it!" Brooke agreed.

"This will keep the family safe," Amanda said. "Victoria's spirit won't be able to get back on the property ever again."

"I'm starving," Dru announced.

"Me too," I said.

Amanda rose to her feet gracefully. "Gabriella told me she'd have food for us waiting when we finished."

Together, we extinguished the candles and gathered up our supplies. Then the four of us walked arm in arm through the now gentle rain, and back to the family wing of the mansion.

CHAPTER TWELVE

The next two weeks passed with no other paranormal issues. Victoria's ghost was long gone as far as I could tell, and finally Gabriella's morning sickness began to ease up. Her appearance improved as she moved into her second trimester, and I watched her getting stronger—and growing bigger—every day.

Chauncey began the renovations on the house he bought, and I was happy and content living at the mansion with Gabriella and her family. Danielle kept me on my toes, but now that Gabriella was feeling better, I was starting to get more free time for myself.

Chauncey and Philippe totally surprised me and offered me the bar manager's position for the event arm of the hotel. I accepted with the understanding that I'd start working right away. Mostly evenings and weekends—basically part-time to start—and slowly I'd work in more hours as Gabriella improved. It was a sweet deal, and I was confident that I could whip the bar into shape. I could literally walk to work, and another perk was being able to spend more time with Chauncey.

Camilla showed up my first day on the job in the bar, while I was counting bottles and logging the inventory, carrying a bouquet of fall flowers from the farmhouse gardens. She was so obviously miserable that I poured her a ginger ale and encouraged her to sit down.

She did her best to make amends. I accepted the flowers and her apology, but things were still a bit strained between us. I made an effort to be polite to her, because while she didn't have the same severity of morning sickness as Gabriella, she still looked exhausted. To her credit, she tried to clear the air, and she apologized again.

After she left, I had to wonder just how badly Victoria had been messing with Camilla's head. Around the same time Camilla had started to act differently toward me, the ghost had been barred from the interior of the mansion. It wasn't an excuse for her previous behavior, but it could be a reason.

Drusilla assured me that Priscilla had done shielding spells on Camilla and warded the Midnight family farmhouse and surrounding property, as well as bolstered the protection to Camilla's shop. So, I figured that would be the end of any Victoria induced problems for Camilla.

Truthfully, I was a tad distracted. There was a lot going on between the new position as bar manager, helping out the family, being with Chauncey, and being the maid-of-honor at Amanda and Zak's upcoming wedding.

Before I knew it, the big day was only hours away. I decided to wear my red dress to the rehearsal dinner and found that I was nervous to meet Amanda's sisters. Her parents, Victor and Susan, I had met previously, but the infamous trouble-making middle sister, Arianna, and the youngest college-aged sister, Angela, I was very curious about.

I had half expected the family of the bride to stay in the mansion's hotel, but Amanda had told me that the four of them were staying together in the casual bed and breakfast in the village.

I suppose I should thank Camilla for the experience of being a bridesmaid. Because now, I knew what to expect. We went through the ceremony rehearsal in the smaller reception room in front of the fireplace—as rain was called for on the wedding day—and I had to admit, I liked the fall flowers and pumpkins all grouped around the hearth and displayed across the mantle.

I was also secretly relieved that Amanda and Zak's wedding was small, only eighty guests, and a dozen of them were the Midnight and Marquette family.

"I'm telling you," I whispered to Amanda, while the officiant spoke to the parents of the bride and groom. "I think I prefer the indoor ceremony by the fireplace as opposed to outside on the terrace. It's cozy and has a moody kind of atmosphere."

"I'm simply going to roll with it." Amanda blew out

a long breath. "I've got enough stress as it is without worrying about getting rained on during the ceremony tomorrow."

"Hey at least you reserved the big penthouse suite for the wedding night," I said. "You two can go upstairs after the reception, and go all sexy, crazy newlywed with each other."

A slow smile spread across the bride's face. "There is that to look forward to. All I have to do is survive the next twenty-four hours."

I aimed a glance over my shoulder where her sisters sat in the front row. "Arianna seems to be behaving herself so far."

Amanda's shoulders tightened.

"Your youngest sister is super cute," I said quickly.

"And blissfully unaware of the family's legacy of Guardianship," Amanda whispered back.

"She's that clueless?"

"I don't think Angela even believes in the paranormal."

"Well, it's a damn good thing we banished Victoria's spirit from the grounds," I said out of the corner of my mouth. "Otherwise, Angela would have gotten one hell of an education while she was here."

Amanda rolled her eyes.

"Personally, I'd pay big money to see her face if Leroy went full Ghostbusters on her."

Now Amanda laughed.

Zak leaned around Amanda and gave me a grin.

"Behave yourself over there, you two."

"Hey, I'm only doing my maid of honor duties and keeping the bride in a good mood," I said.

The next evening, I stood by Amanda's side before the stone fireplace as she and Zakary Parker exchanged their vows. The fire crackled in the grate, gorgeous fall flowers decorated the mantle, and pumpkins and pots of orange mums were stacked strategically around the edges of the hearth.

Amanda's gown was beaded, mostly gold, and cut in the mermaid style. Sheer sleeves were embellished with more golden beads and sequins, and they ended at her elbows. It had a boat neckline and illusion top, but the back was solid—which neatly hid all of her protective, magickal tattoos. The skirt was long, and the beading lessened toward the bottom revealing ivory tulle.

Zak and his best man wore deep brown tuxes, with crisp white shirts and burnt orange ties that matched the color of my dress. I held her flowers and mine while the couple exchanged rings and sealed the deal with a kiss. They were introduced as Mr. and Mrs. Parker for the first time, and I passed back her bouquet, a pretty cluster of fall leaves and roses.

Dru had gone on and on about the meanings of the flowers, but I simply liked them. The hand-tied bridal bouquet was filled with ivory, chocolate brown, and different shades of orange roses. The flowers were surrounded by fall foliage, and it smelled terrific.

I waited with Zak's brother and then took his arm,

and we moved down the short aisle and out with the bride and groom to form a receiving line.

An hour later, the reception was hopping. Music pumped out of the speakers and the guests were enjoying themselves at the bar and out on the dance floor. I worked my way to the bar to check in and see how things were going. Jaxon had a smile on his face and was working his tail off. I offered to give him a hand, but he insisted he was fine. I gave him a thumb's up and waited with Chauncey while he ordered two bottles of wine for our family table and ginger ale for Gabriella and Camilla.

"You look beautiful tonight," Chauncey said.

I wiggled my eyebrows at him. "Yes, I'll sleep with you."

He grinned. "The most gorgeous maid-of-honor I've ever seen."

"Turns out I don't look too bad in burnt orange." I smiled. "Don't forget to order a Dr. Pepper for Brooke."

I spotted Amanda's youngest sister. She was out on the dance floor with Amanda, and they were dancing. Amanda was smiling, and her youngest sister was adorable. Angela had brown hair, with copper undertones similar to Amanda's, but she had the stereotypical bouncy energy of a college co-ed.

Arianna, I noted, was quiet and very reserved, and I was relieved to see, also still on her best behavior. She sipped at a sparkling water and had stayed at her parent's table the entire evening so far. She'd refused a few offers to dance, but she'd been polite about it.

Arianna looked like a damn movie star, I decided. The sort of woman who drew stares no matter where she went. Her dark hair tumbled around her shoulders, and she was poured into a low cut, black mini dress that left little to the imagination. While I was no fashion critic, the dress struck me as inappropriate to wear to her sister's wedding.

Yet despite that, I'd never seen a more stunning woman. Maybe she felt my appraisal, because abruptly she turned her head and our eyes met.

I pointed two fingers towards my own eyes and back toward Arianna, in the classic *I'm watching you* gesture.

Inclining her head slightly, she acknowledged the warning.

"Estella," Chauncey said, accepting the bottles from Jaxon. "Are you still giving Amanda's sister the stink-eye?'

"You're damn right I am," I said cheerfully. "Amanda asked me to make sure Arianna didn't cause a scene."

"And here I thought, when I saw you speaking to her at the rehearsal last night, that you were simply being friendly."

I smirked at him and picked up the tray with the soft drinks one-handed. "It's adorable that you thought so."

"Did you threaten her?" he asked.

"*Threaten* is a strong word." I fluttered my eyelashes at him.

"Jesus." Chauncey shook his head. "You did."

I smiled, thinking back to the night before...

When we had been introduced, I had not offered my hand. Instead, I took the opportunity to put Arianna on notice. "I've heard a lot about you," I said.

She smiled ruefully. "I'm sure you have."

"Amanda is my best friend," I said softly. "I won't see her special day ruined, *comprende*?"

"Yes, I understand." Arianna nodded her head. "I'd never dream of spoiling things for her."

"I'm here to make sure that you won't." I smiled and kept my voice low. "If I see *anything* I don't like, I'm coming for you, Arianna. And I will personally take great satisfaction in forcibly removing you from the building."

"So ferocious," she said with a light laugh.

"Try me," I said. "Please."

Arianna's eyes had gone wide, and she'd glanced away from me quickly. She'd avoided me for the rest of the evening, and best of all, she stayed in the background doing nothing to attract attention to herself.

The truth was her sitting quietly by her parents' side at the reception said one thing. However, her *Hey sailor!* outfit said quite another.

At any rate, things were under control for the moment, so I gave Chauncey a friendly hip bump. "What do you say we drop off these drinks and then you and I go hit the dance floor?"

He cocked his head to one side. "Did you just ask

me to dance?"

"I did."

"I'd love to," he said. "It will be nice to dance with you at a wedding for once, and not have you scowl at me."

I glared at him. "I did not scowl at you. Well, no more than you deserved."

He started to chuckle. "God, I'm crazy about you." He dipped his head and spoke close to my ear. "After the wedding reception is over, maybe we can go check out one of the hotel suites...I happen to know one of them is vacant."

"Very smooth, Marquette," I said.

"You know you love that about me." He nipped my ear.

"Yup." I pressed a kiss to his mouth. "Turns out that I do."

***

When all was said and done, the wedding reception had gone beautifully. We sent Amanda and Zak off on their honeymoon the next day, and I was relieved to see them drive away from the mansion while the family waved and wished them well.

Chauncey slipped his arm around my waist as we walked back toward the hotel side of the mansion. "I was going to go by the house tonight; see how the renovations are progressing in the kitchen and upstairs baths."

"Did you exorcise the patriotic cat demons?" I asked hopefully.

"You'll have to come over and see for yourself."

"I have some paperwork to finish up first, and liquor orders to go over, but I can be free after four."

We walked along the hall and stopped in front of his office. "We need to see about getting you a real office of your own," Chauncey said.

"I don't need a formal office. I can easily work from the bar."

"Come here," he said, tugging me close. "I want to kiss you."

"Not while we're at work." I eased back. "Since you manage the hotel, you're basically my *boss*."

"I don't care who sees us."

"I do," I said. "I don't want the staff thinking I got this job because I'm sleeping with you."

Chauncey frowned. "Anyone who's seen all the hard work you've put in in the past week would never think that."

I didn't agree but instead of arguing, I smiled. "See you at four?"

He gave me a long, considering look. "Yes," he finally said. "You will."

I was able to finish up by three, and that gave me enough time to dash upstairs and check in with Gabriella. She'd finally felt good enough to go back to her freelance job of designing book covers and sat at her desk in the tower room working on a new design. Her pale blonde hair curled all around her head and down her back. She was humming to herself and working away.

I caught a glimpse of the cover art and grinned. It was a sexy looking historical romance cover. Of course, there was a big clinch. The man smoldered and the woman had her head thrown back with a whole lot of cleavage showing.

"Damn, Sis. That's a lot of heaving bosoms," I joked, but got no response.

I called her name, and when she didn't react, I dropped my hand on her shoulder. "Hey, Gabriella."

"Ack!" She jumped straight up into the air and then fumbled for the noise cancelling headphones she wore and pulled them off her head.

"Sorry!" I laughed. "I didn't see the headphones. They were hidden in your curls."

"By the goddess." She patted a hand to her chest. "You scared me."

"Where's everybody?"

"Dru took Danielle to her house for the night and Philippe was meeting with Garrett and Nicole. Something about a few new varieties of wine before the holidays."

"I wanted to let you know that I won't be here for supper tonight. Chauncey and I are going out."

"Reeeally?" Gabriella drew out the word and wiggled her eyebrows. "Anywhere romantic?"

"Yeah. We're going to his house to see how the kitchen reno and the bathroom plumbing is coming along. It's gonna be super sexy."

"I'm glad to see you and Chauncey finally together." Gabriella sat back in her chair and sent me a smile. "I mean the way you both snarled and sniffed around each other for the past year has been entertaining to watch, but I was about to resort to brewing a love potion to kick you two up to the line."

My jaw dropped. "I thought there were rules against love potions? Isn't that considered to be manipulative?"

"Well..." she said. "There's rules and then there are *rules*."

My jaw dropped. "Can I say how relieved I am that you managed to restrain yourself?"

Playfully, she stuck her nose in the air. "As well you should be."

"Damn good thing I've been doing most of the cooking around here..."

Gabriella grinned. "Go on, get out of here, and know that I'll expect a full report when you get back."

"On the plumbing?"

"No," she said, "on how you two had crazy sex all over *every* available flat surface in that empty house."

I rolled my eyes. "Very funny."

"You're not coming back early, are you?" she asked.

"Er, no. Why?"

"Well with Danielle at Dru's, and you out with Chauncey, Philippe promised to bring home a pizza tonight. We're having a date night."

"And *you* want to go crazy on every available flat surface in the family wing, is that it?"

Gabriella sighed. "A girl can dream."

I pointed my finger at her. "If I come home and find out you are having triplets instead of twins, I'm not going to take that very well."

"Ha!" Gabriella said.

"Have fun!" she called after me as I walked down the hall.

"You too!" I called back.

***

Chauncey was acting stressed when he picked me up. He was holding himself differently, and when I asked him what was wrong, he nervously flinched. I watched him out of my peripheral and wondered what had gotten into him. Maybe that comment I'd made about not wanting the hotel staff to think I'd gotten my job by sleeping with him had finally sunk in.

Had I hurt his feelings? *Aw shit,* I thought. *I'm not any good at this relationship stuff. I need to try harder.* Determined to make sure he knew that I truly cared about him, I threw myself into a discussion of the best color for kitchen cabinets.

He was all excited about the house. So, when we walked in to check out the progress made on the kitchen, I figured I simply needed to show a little more interest and have an opinion. Which it ended up wasn't hard. The poor man was thinking of going with plain white cabinets.

"No way," I argued as he held up an array of wall paint colors. "Don't do white cabinets. Everyone and their brother has an all white kitchen. You need a darker color in here, something to play off that newly exposed and gorgeous stone wall."

"What would you suggest?" he said.

I grabbed the paint chips and held them up to the unpainted base cabinets. "I like this dark green, or *ooh*, this deep blue is pretty too!" Then, I walked over to the board of samples of countertops the contractor had left for him. "This counter. It's got similar colors as the stone wall, but it's made from quartz." I picked it up and carried it over to the cabinets. "Amanda says that's tougher, holds up to abuse, and is easier to clean."

He moved to stand next to me. "Well, if it's going to be in *this* kitchen, it had better be sturdy. Especially as you and I have a tendency to defile kitchen countertops."

I narrowed one eye. "Was that a joke?"

"No," he said. "I'm very serious."

Nervously, I cleared my throat. "Maybe we should go upstairs and look at all the plumbing work."

He brushed the hair from the nape of my neck and began to nibble.

"I, ah." I cleared my throat. "We were talking about cabinet colors and countertops."

"Keep talking," he said. "For some strange reason, I got very turned on as soon as you mentioned countertops."

I chuckled and it slid into a groan as he ran his tongue up to my ear. I stared unseeing out the kitchen window, as he whispered a very naughty suggestion to me.

"Well, you're in an adventurous mood," I said.

He began to gnaw on my neck, and his hands raced all over me. With a shudder, I reached out to hold myself steady against the cabinet. In fact, I was so preoccupied that it took me a moment to focus on what I was seeing across the side yard of his property and over in Amanda's backyard.

"What's *that*?" I asked, staring out the window.

With a chuckle he pressed against my backside. "I think you know..."

"Stop that," I said distractedly. "Chauncey, look out the window. Is that Angela? Amanda's sister?"

I narrowed my eyes as Angela drug a large wooden box across the grass, and then I jumped when she promptly started beating the hell out of it with a hammer.

"My love! My love!" Angela screamed. "Come back to me!"

"What is she *doing*?" I said, leaning father over the cabinets and closer to the window. Pieces of wood were flying, and Angela was crying and swinging the hammer wildly.

"Chauncey," I said, "are you seeing this?"

Suddenly Chauncey clamped his arms around me. It wasn't playful. It wasn't sexy. It was painful.

"*Mon couer,*" he said, and his voice was different and accented. He began muttering in French, and my stomach dropped. This wasn't Chauncey who held me...not anymore. It was Pierre-Michel.

"Let go!" I demanded.

But Pierre-Michel didn't let go, in fact he laughed and squeezed me even harder.

I fought against his suffocating hold as hard as I could, but my arms were pinned at my side. I was considering slamming my head back but didn't want to break Chauncey's nose. I knew he was still in there.

Pierre-Michel laughed again and started to lift me off my feet. When he did, his grip slipped up higher on my arms. It was all the opportunity that I needed. Swinging my right hand back, I slapped open handed at his crotch, three times. He dropped me to my feet immediately and bent over, groaning in pain.

I didn't wait to see what Pierre-Michel would do next, I shot out the kitchen door and rushed to Amanda's house.

Angela was screaming hysterically. Somehow, she had found the crate that Amanda had put Pierre-Michel's cursed portrait in. As I ran closer, I saw her ripping at pieces of wood with her bare hands. She tore chunks of boards off like they were no more than cardboard.

"Angela, stop!" I shouted.

"Pierre-Michel!" she screamed, tearing into the wood with more strength than a mortal should naturally have. "My love! I will set you free!"

I gained Amanda's backyard and now saw that the portrait was completely revealed. I skidded to a stop a few feet away from her. Angela still held the hammer and when her eyes met mine, I recoiled.

"Where is he?" she snarled. Her voice was magnified, deeper, and her eyes were wild.

Angela Beaumont was no longer at home, because I was staring straight into the insane face of Victoria Midnight.

CHAPTER THIRTEEN

"Where is Pierre-Michel?" she demanded again.

"I slapped his balls up to his throat," I said. "I'm afraid he's not going to be doing you any good for a while."

With a primal scream, she threw the hammer at me. I managed to dodge it, barely.

Still, she'd done exactly what I hoped she'd do. She had thrown away her weapon. Now it was down to her and me. "Victoria, let her go," I said, as I began to circle around the remains of the crate. "Angela is only a kid."

"No!" She tossed her head. "She is descended from both me and Pierre-Michel, therefore she is mine to use as I see fit."

"You've got a screwed-up version of family, Victoria." I moved a bit closer and was fairly certain I could take her, but then Victoria—in Angela's body—lunged at me much faster than I'd expected.

Her fingers were curled into claws as she rushed

forward; left with no other options I threw a punch. My fist connected with her jaw. Her head snapped back, and she fell straight back on the grass. She was out cold.

"Hey!" An outraged shout came from behind me. "You *bitch*! Leave my sister alone!"

I saw motion from my peripheral and was grabbed by a brunette woman.

"Arianna!" I grabbed her hands as she tried to slap me. Moving fast, I twisted her arm up and behind her back. "Stop! That's *not* Angela! She's possessed!"

Arianna swore and struggled.

"God damn it," I snarled as we fought. "Don't make me knock you out too! I'm going to need your help. Angela *is* possessed!"

Arianna froze. "What did you say?"

I didn't have a chance to answer, because suddenly Angela/Victoria sat straight up. It was like something out of a horror movie. Slowly, her head twisted, and she regarded Arianna and me with a terrifying smile.

"By the goddess." Arianna gasped. "Angela?"

"Where is my love?" Angela/Victoria demanded in that louder, enhanced voice. "You won't keep him from me any longer!"

I let go of Arianna and the two of us spun to face the spirit.

"Victoria!" a male voice bellowed from the direction of Chauncey's house.

"Aw *shit*," I said. "We just ran out of time."

"What do you mean?" Arianna said.

"We can't let your sister and Chauncey get together; the consequences could be very bad."

"Define *bad*!" Arianna demanded.

"We have to get the spirit out of Angela. The last time one of these ghosts possessed someone for an extended period of time, they landed in the hospital. We need help! The only person I ever saw yank a spirit out of someone, just left for her honeymoon."

"You need my father," Arianna said. "He trained Amanda."

"How long to get him here?"

"Five minutes, maybe?"

"Let's get your sister in the house before Pierre-Michel figures out where she is," I said.

Arianna nodded and together we rushed Angela. Each grabbing her by one arm, we drug her inside of Amanda's house as she kicked and screamed.

The door slammed shut behind us.

"Lock down!" Arianna shouted, and the house sprang to life, heeding her command.

A length of rope suddenly appeared on the counter. Arianna and I nodded to each other and strong-armed Angela/Victoria into the chair. It was harder tying her to the wooden kitchen chair than it had been getting her inside.

Once she was secure, Arianna pulled her phone from the pocket of her jeans. "Dad?" she said into the phone. "It's bad. It's Angie, we're at Amanda's house—"

Angela/Victoria began to scream in rage. It was horrible to hear.

"Yes, that's her," Arianna said. "Spirit possession. Stage three."

Arianna disconnected. "He's on the way." She focused on her sister, simultaneously working a complicated gesture with her hands. "Silence!" Arianna commanded, and instantly Victoria's spirit stopped screaming through Angela.

"Whoa!" I considered the brunette. "Well, damn girl, clearly you know your magicks."

"Amanda wasn't the only Beaumont trained in magick," Arianna said. "She was simply better at it."

"I'm not complaining," I said. "All we have to do is hold out for—"

A loud thud sounded at the kitchen door.

"*Victoria!*" Pierre-Michel shouted and threw himself against the door, trying to get inside. When that didn't work, he picked up a terra cotta pot and threw it at the kitchen window.

I cringed away from the window, but while the pot shattered and the window glass spider-webbed, the window promptly healed itself.

"Wow," I said, amazed.

"He'll never get in here," Arianna said.

"You have to let me go." The voice was quiet, calm, and reasonable, and it came from Angela/Victoria. "Our torture will never end until we can finally join our spirits together."

"Glad you calmed down, Victoria," I said. "But that's still a hard *no* from me."

"Please." Suddenly it was Angela's voice. "Arianna, I can't hold out against her much longer."

"Angela?" Arianna asked as the girl's chin dropped to her chest.

Angela's head snapped back up, and it was Victoria's voice once again. "Once we touch, the curse will be broken. You can end our torment."

"Chauncey and I were ridden by Victoria and Pierre-Michel before," I said to Arianna. "We—I mean they—made us kiss. It didn't end the curse."

"It wasn't enough," Victoria said. "We both have to be where the curse originated from *and* profess our love."

"No way it's that easy," I said.

"Maybe it is," Arianna said. "Love *is* the most powerful force on the planet."

I thought about it. "Louisa most likely cast the original curse here, from her home..."

"At last, you see. Please. *Please*, release me," Victoria pleaded softly.

"Fine," Arianna nodded. "But you'll take me, I'll be the conduit."

"No!" I shouted.

"You do this willingly?" Victoria asked.

"Leave my sister's body and take mine," Arianna said. "Do it now."

"Agreed," Victoria said.

"No! Arianna, don't invite the spirit in!" I said, but it was too late.

Angela's head fell back and from her mouth poured an illuminated form. It whirled around Arianna, looking for a way to gain entrance. "Keep Angela safe," Arianna said to me, and then she relaxed her body. With a soft exhale, she closed her eyes and gave herself up to the spirit of Victoria Midnight.

I watched as Victoria's spirit filled her up. Arianna's dark hair swirled all around her face as the spirit claimed her. Slowly, Arianna opened her eyes and walked toward the door. "Unlock," she said calmly, and the door swung open.

Chauncey stood in the doorway. His hair was wild, and his face was not quite his own. It was almost as if he were wearing a younger, thinner version of himself as a mask. Arianna walked directly to him, and she reached up to frame his face with her hands.

"*Je t'aime pour toujour, Pierre-Michel,*" she said.

"Victoria," Pierre-Michel said. "*Je t'aime.*"

Pierre-Michel and Victoria kissed. A glow appeared around the couple, and a spectral wind whistled through the door and into the kitchen. It was strong enough to have their clothes ruffling and hair billowing around their faces.

They pulled apart and Victoria smiled up into Pierre-Michel's face. "I know you were innocent of the crime you were accused of. Our son is safe—with great-great grandchildren of his own, and I have waited for you for centuries."

Pierre-Michel rested his forehead against hers. "You believing in me is all the magick I have ever needed."

Victoria smiled. "Let us go home."

They kissed again and an explosion of bright light showed all around the couple. It was so bright I shielded my eyes. The light dimmed and two new lights, like shooting stars, burst forth from their bodies.

Chauncey and Arianna promptly collapsed. He crumbled onto the deck, and she sort of melted to the kitchen floor. I leapt forward to check on them and found they were both still breathing. Looking up, I watched the two lights rise upwards. The lights were circling around each other and slowly moving higher and higher into the darkening sky.

"Arianna! Angela!" Victor Beaumont's voice sounded from behind me. He skidded to a stop on the back deck of Amanda's home. "Spirit lights," he said, watching with me as those two lights moved higher and farther away. And then suddenly, they were gone.

"Blessed be," I murmured. It seemed like the most appropriate thing to say. Beside me on the deck, Chauncey groaned and moved.

"Estella, you and Arianna were supposed to wait for me," Victor said.

"Sorry Vic." I gave him a smile, as I bent to check on Chauncey. "I tried, but Arianna went all hero on me and the next thing you know..."

Victor moved to the doorway and spotted his

daughters in the kitchen. One was semi-conscious on the floor and the other was crying and tied to the kitchen chair.

"Dad? What in the hell happened?" Angela demanded. "Were those ghosts or something?"

"Yes, they were," he said.

"Estella?" Chauncey squinted at me and tried to sit up. "I feel like I was hit by a truck."

"You were hit by the spirit of Pierre-Michel," I said. "He took you for a ride again."

"Why am I tied up?" Angela struggled against the restraints. "Somebody tell me what's going on!"

"Sit tight," Victor said to Angela. "I want to check on your sister."

Chauncey propped his shoulder against the side of the house. "Go untie her, I'm just going to sit here for a minute."

"Estella?" Angela squirmed in the chair. "What happened to me?"

I walked to the girl. "Long story short, Angela? You were possessed by a whacked out, lovesick, ghost named Victoria Midnight. You tore apart a protected crate and freed her cursed lover from an enchanted painting."

Angela's breath whooshed out. "I sort of remember doing that. But how can that be? There's no such thing as ghosts, curses, and magick," she said in a small voice.

I snorted out a laugh. "Whatever helps you sleep at

night." I untied the rope and it fell to the floor. "By the way, sorry I punched you. It wasn't personal. You weren't yourself at the time."

Angela ran a hand over her jaw. "Did Victoria...I mean, did *I* try to hurt you?" she asked, sounding horrified.

"Yes, *she* did," I said, helping her stand up. "It's okay Angela, I know you didn't mean it. You were simply along for the ride, like Chauncey was."

"Well, I'm not sure what exactly happened, but I'm sorry about attacking you, Estella. I'm glad you stopped me."

Victor was checking Arianna's pulse. "We're going to need some magickal help with all of this. Do you know any good healers, Estella?"

"As a matter of fact, I do." I went straight to the phone on Amanda's counter and called my grandmother.

"Hi Gran," I said, when she answered the phone. "I'm going to need you to go full on wise woman with the magickal remedies and help a few folks out."

"Where are you?" she asked.

"Wise woman?" Angela asked the room in general.

I filled in my grandmother as quickly as possible and hung up. Then I went straight to Chauncey. "Come on," I said, helping him to his feet.

He staggered. "I got it," he said, and held himself up by using the doorframe. "God, how I *hate* spirit possession."

Angela's eyes went comically large in her face. "Oh. My. God. I feel like I'm in the twilight zone."

"Make that the daughters of Midnight zone," I said, helping Chauncey forward.

***

Not only did my grandmother show up, but so did Camilla. Victor called his wife, and I thought to call Leroy. The old man showed up with his usual bag of tricks and promptly went about taking readings and documenting the paranormal event.

We turned Amanda's living room into a magickal triage of sorts. I did what I could to help...setting out healing crystals, lighting candles and protective incense. Susan bustled around brewing tea and pushing cookies on the possession victims. Seems that after being married to a Guardian, Susan knew all about psychic first aid.

"We need to get their blood sugar back up," she told me with a wink.

I nodded and tossed ice cubes in two separate freezer bags, and then wrapped them in thin dish towels, making ice packs. One for Chauncey's groin and another for Angela's jaw.

Arianna sat in a chair. She was tired, but otherwise doing okay. Angela, being possessed the longest, was flat on her back on the sofa. She kept firing off questions at her parents.

"Let me get this straight," Angela said, accepting the ice pack from me. "Thanks, Estella."

"Hold that on your jaw," I suggested.

"Right." She pressed it against the bruise that was forming there and hissed. "Where was I?" she asked me.

"You were finding out about our Guardian heritage," Arianna said from across the room.

"Oh, right." She nodded. "So, our whole family does magick, and Amanda fights supernatural bad guys— because Dad has retired from doing it— and you and Mom decided to keep this all a secret from me for my *entire life*?"

"Angela." My grandmother laid her hand on the young woman's head. "I need you to be quiet for a few moments while I work a healing on you. The astral injuries to your aura are severe. I need to concentrate."

"Astral injuries?" Angela was clearly confused.

"Think of it like the energy field all around your body," I explained. "It has had holes poked in it, from what happened today. My grandmother is going to patch them up."

Angela simply gaped at me.

"Roll with it kid," I suggested.

I walked to Chauncey, who sat in a club chair while Camilla stood behind him sensing the energy field above his head and shoulders.

"You have an injury at your root chakra, Chauncey," she said. "It's not a severe injury but quite painful.

216

What happened?"

"Here you go." I handed him the ice pack. "Use this on your, er, root chakra."

He said nothing but took the ice pack and applied it.

"Sorry about that," I murmured.

Camilla's jaw dropped. "*You* did that to him?"

"Not to *him*," I corrected her. "I defended myself from an overly horny Pierre-Michel."

"How will I ever apologize to you for that?" Chauncey asked me.

"It wasn't really you," I pointed out. "He took you over."

Chauncey grimaced. "Regardless, I am deeply sorry, Estella."

I folded my arms over my chest. "Look if I were you, I'd be more concerned about how annoyed I was watching the man I love kissing Arianna."

His eyes flashed worriedly to mine, and I started to chuckle.

Camilla smiled. "Excuse me for a moment. I need to gather some more healing crystals for Chauncey." With a pat to his shoulder and a wink to me, she walked away and gave us a bit of privacy.

"Chauncey." I knelt down in front of his chair. "I'm simply relieved that this whole star-crossed ghost thing is over. Now their spirits have moved on, and everyone is safe. You and me? We're good."

"I love you," he said quietly. "And again, I'm sorry."

"I love you, Chauncey," I said, taking his free hand.

"We won't let those crazy ghosts ruin this for us, will we?"

"Not bloody likely," Chauncey said.

"There you go," I said and leaned forward to kiss him.

***

Nothing was ruined between us. As a couple we were just fine. Better than fine, in fact. Chauncey was uncomfortable for a few days, but he recovered—and very nicely too I might add.

Susan, Arianna, and Angela departed for Florida. Arianna was fine, simply a little tired, and Susan and my grandmother were well on their way to becoming fast friends. Angela was as good as new except for a bruised jaw, and she went home with a couple of beginner level books on magick—thanks to Camilla.

I promised Angela that I would have Amanda send her a good reading list, once she returned from her honeymoon. Angela and I exchanged phone numbers and email addresses and I had to admit, I liked that kid.

We had all decided together not to interrupt the newlyweds. I promised Victor that I would fill Amanda in on everything when she and Zak came back from their wedding trip. Victor agreed, yet still, he stayed behind in Ames Crossing for a few more days after Susan and the girls left. For *clean up*, he said.

He and Leroy decided that the old painting should be

destroyed, and so they ritually burned it *and* the crate it had been held in. They used the fire pit in Amanda's back yard, and I stood by their side as the old portrait burned. While Victor worked his magick, I tossed the pieces of the crate into the fire and added handfuls of protective herbs from Amanda's gardens.

Together the three of us watched the smoke billow up to the stars. Once everything was reduced to ashes, Leroy tested the remains with his equipment and found no traces of paranormal energy.

Victor took it a step farther and scooped up all the ashes into metal buckets. He salted them for good measure, and then I accompanied him as he went to bury the ashes.

Victor used an old cemetery on the cliffs. It felt very surreal to be trudging through a graveyard at midnight, toting buckets and shovels with a former Guardian; but I was honored to be there. We buried the ashes within the boundaries of the cemetery, inside the gate and well clear of any graves.

Working with Victor that night had taught me quite a lot. He says that I'll make a fine assistant for Amanda. He departed for Florida the next morning, and I gave him a hug and promised to keep in touch.

After the Beaumonts left, the following week was quiet. It took me a while to realize that I'd never known a time where I wasn't looking over my shoulder and expecting some sort of ghostly trouble.

Chauncey's house renovation was coming right

along, and so finally, we tried again for a date night at his old stone house to check on the progress.

Chauncey had brought along a quilt, and we spread it on the hardwood floor, in front of the fireplace in the living room. It was a bit chilly outside, so we built a small fire and used the stone hearth for a table. We sat side by side eating hamburgers and fries and Chauncey surprised me by breaking out an unlabeled bottle of wine.

"Ooh, la la," I said. "Fancy wine and fast-food burgers. It's very *us*."

"Can you handle wine in a plastic cup?" he asked.

"Of course." I tugged my denim jacket closer to stay warm. "I'm not exactly the crystal goblet type."

He smiled and poured the pale golden wine. "I think you'll like this vintage."

"How come it doesn't have a label?" I asked.

"This is one of the new varieties from *Trois Amis*," he said, handing me a glass. "What do you think?"

I took a sip, and let it sit on my tongue. "Nice. Not too sweet, not too dry. In fact, I like it." I took another sip. "This will be a popular one with the guests at the events at the mansion."

"I agree," Chauncey said. "Philippe and Garrett believe it will be an excellent addition to the wine list for the *Trois Aims* winery in the new year."

"What are they going to call this one?" I sipped again. "Or are they still debating the name? Because last I heard they still haven't chosen the name for that new spiced wine for the holidays."

"This one was easier. The name was unanimous between the three friends."

"You mean Garrett, Philippe, *and* Brooke all agreed on a name?"

"They did," Chauncey said. "With some input from me. It's going to be called, *Ètoile Brillante.*"

"Oh, that's French. Eh-twall..." I tried to pronounce it and failed, miserably. "What's that mean, anyway?"

"It means bright star," Chauncey said.

My jaw dropped. "Really?"

"We all decided the wine should be named after you."

"Why would you do that?" I asked, flabbergasted.

"Because you are our brave and bright shining star."

"Damn it. Don't make me cry," I said, doing my best not to tear up.

Chauncey smiled and shifted from sitting beside me, to being on one knee.

"What are you doing?" I asked, as my heart slammed against my ribs.

"I had planned to do this the last time we were here, but our evening got a little—"

"Hijacked?" I finished for him.

He pulled a small box out of his leather jacket pocket.

"Estella, I love you."

My eyes grew large in my face, and I sat there silently as he opened the box.

"Marry me," he said, revealing a diamond ring.

I looked at the ring and gasped. The center stone was held in a halo setting. Smaller diamonds created the five points of a star, and it was all set in white gold.

"It's a star," I breathed, and didn't move a muscle.

"Do you like it?"

Overcome, I could only nod as tears rolled down my face.

He smiled. "Is that a yes?"

"Yes." I nodded again and held out my left hand.

Chauncey pulled the ring from the box and slipped it on my finger.

"It's the most beautiful ring I've ever seen," I said, staring at the diamond. "I love it."

"I love you," he said. "I want to build a life with you here in this house. Create new, happy memories and have a family."

I lifted my eyes to his. "I love you. I also want to build new memories and have a bunch of kids with you, here in this old house." I blew out a shaky breath. "Maybe coincidence and two ghosts kept throwing us together at the start of all of this, but in the end, I chose you and you chose me. I always knew deep down that you were my destiny, Chauncey Marquette."

"Damn it," he said. "Don't make *me* cry."

We both began to laugh, reaching for each other at the same time. We kissed, and after a moment, I tugged him down with me to the quilt. Together, we rolled over the blanket, neither of us caring about the hardwood floor.

"When?" he asked, as we pulled the clothes from each other. "When do you want to get married?"

"Next summer?" I said, dragging his shirt over his head

"Summer?" he asked.

"It'd be best to wait until after the babies are all born." I gasped as he ran his hands over me, and I promptly lost my entire train of thought.

Afterward, we lay in front of the fire, mostly on the quilt. Chauncey snuggled closer and flipped a corner of the quilt over us.

I caught myself staring at my ring. It seemed like such a silly, girly thing to do, and honestly? I didn't care.

"How do you feel about a small ceremony in the walled gardens of the mansion?" I asked.

"In the spot where we first met?" he asked.

"Exactly," I said and kissed him.

"So, your secret is out: you're actually a romantic." He grinned as he said it. "I love that idea."

"I'll want to keep our wedding *small*." I leaned up on one elbow to look in his dark brown eyes. "And not too fancy. I'd want to wear a short dress. The big billowy gown thing is not my style. Are you okay with the idea of a simple ceremony and reception?"

"I like the idea of doing something more intimate," he said, running his hand through my hair.

"I love you." I sighed happily and wriggled closer.

"And I love you." He drew me back down to him.
I smiled. "Show me how much."
And he did.

EPILOGUE

We held our wedding ceremony in the walled gardens of the Marquette mansion, where we'd first met. It was a mild June afternoon, and purple coneflowers, yellow yarrow, herbs, and roses bloomed all around us. I chose Amanda as my matron of honor and only attendant, and Chauncey had chosen Zak to stand as his best man.

We had kept the guest list small, with my grandmother, Chauncey's grandfather, my three sisters and their families, and Amanda's parents and sisters. We also included Leroy, and Max and Nicole Dubois and their son. Our reception dinner would be held in one of the smaller, more intimate reception rooms at the mansion.

I stood with Amanda in the shade of a pop-up canopy at the back of the garden as the guests took their seats. Drusilla and Garrett sat with Brooke, Abby, and Alex. Camilla sat beside Dru's family with her stepson, Jaime. Jacob, Camilla's husband, sat on the other side of Jaime and held their four-week-old daughter, Jasmine, over his shoulder.

Across the aisle Gabriella sat with Henri Marquette, Danielle, and Gran. Between Gran and Gabriella—in lieu of a chair—was a twin stroller. Somehow, we'd lucked out and the twins, Archer and Celeste, were both sound asleep.

Behind them sat Amanda's family, and I saw Susan lean forward and whisper to my grandmother. Angela was happily looking at the flowers in the gardens, and Arianna was sitting and talking to Victor. I nodded, relieved that there'd be no shortage of helping hands if Danielle got antsy, or if one of the almost three-month-old twins woke during the ceremony.

Leroy, that old rascal, was entertaining Caleb, Max and Nicole's son; and as I watched, Leroy began to bounce Caleb on his knee.

Even though I was relieved to see the family all in place, I still found that I was *extremely* nervous, and I hadn't expected to be. I took a deep breath and slowly blew it out, telling myself to calm down. I was surrounded by the daughters of Midnight: my three sisters, and my three cousins, Amanda, Arianna, and Angela. They'd never let anything go wrong on Chauncey's and my special day.

Beside me, Amanda reached for my hand. "I couldn't believe it when you told me you were going to wear a short wedding dress," she said. "It's perfect for a garden wedding, and you look incredibly *chic,* Estella."

"Thank you," I said, smoothing a hand over the dress. My wedding dress was simple and made from white eyelash lace over a nude-colored lining. It had short fluttering sleeves that lay delicately against my skin. The neckline was round, and the bodice was fitted with a slightly flared skirt. The sassy scalloped hem ended four inches above my knees.

To compliment the summer dress, I wore nude strappy sandals with low, wide heels that would allow me to better navigate the garden pathway and grass. I'd left my hair down and loose, with only a tiny floral crown of ivory rose buds. For my bouquet, Drusilla had put together flowers from the gardens. The plume-looking flowers in peach, cream and other pastel shades were called astilbe, she'd told me. Dru had handed me the bouquet, brushed a kiss over my cheek, and explained that the flowers meant that 'love was worth the wait.'

From one side of the garden, the string quartet began to play, and I blinked, the music taking me from my thoughts over the magickal language of flowers.

Amanda smiled. "Pachelbel's Canon," she said reverently. "That's perfect."

"Figured you would know what the song was." I smiled at her. She'd also left her hair down today, and looked lovely in a fitted, short, peach-colored matron-of-honor dress.

"Blessed be." Wishing me luck, she pressed her cheek to mine and headed off to go start the procession.

"Ready, *ma cher*?" Philippe asked.

I took his arm. "Thank you for walking me down the aisle," I said softly.

"It is my great pleasure," he said, patting my hand.

Philippe was very dapper in his creamy-beige summer suit. He wore no tie—none of the men in the wedding party were—and their crisp white dress shirts were unbuttoned at the throat, as Chauncey and I wanted to keep it casual but still festive.

Philippe paused, somehow knowing when the correct time was to begin, and we started down the garden path/wedding aisle while the musicians continued to play. Chauncey had suggested the string quartet, and suddenly I was glad that I had agreed. It was very romantic.

Unexpectedly, the music hit me in the feels. I struggled not to cry and smiled instead as I caught sight of Chauncey, who was waiting for me under an arbor draped with cream and peach-colored roses for love and enchantment and green ivy for fidelity.

Chauncey smiled back at me, and I was struck all over again at how incredibly handsome he was. *Just look at him,* I thought. *Standing beneath the roses, that summer beige suit setting off his dark hair, and he is waiting...for me.*

My nerves vanished, and I walked happily towards him and our new life. As I took my place beside him, we clasped hands and I turned to him with a smile.

The future was bright with a whole magickal world

of loving possibilities and whatever destiny we would create for ourselves.

The End

ABOUT THE AUTHOR

Ellen Dugan is the award-winning author of over thirty-nine books. Ellen's non-fiction titles have been translated into over twelve foreign languages. She branched out successfully into fiction with her popular *Legacy Of Magick, The Gypsy Chronicles, Daughters Of Midnight,* and *Hemlock Hollow* series. Ellen has been featured in USA TODAY'S HEA column. She lives an enchanted life in Missouri tending to her extensive perennial gardens and writing. Please visit her website or social media:

www.ellendugan.com
www.facebook.com/ellendugan
www.instagram.com/ellendugan/

Made in the USA
Monee, IL
19 November 2021